Other books by the author

Solscapes

Solscapes Volume II: We Spell it Mythral

Stalkers

Coming in 2022

GAIA 2.0

Solscapes Volume IV: The Truth of the Taint

Solscapes Volume III:

The ¢o$t of Money

By M. S. M. Atwood

SolscapesMultiverse.com

To my dog

CONTENTS

CHAPTER 1: JUST TO CONFUSE YOU, ASSHOLE

"We did it! Dr. K says there's only a slight chance that we've also murdered everyone everywhere." Huck Lotterydale's voice comes out of Benkle's phone. Benkle turns baggy eyes to his clock. 2AM. His alarm is going to go off in three hours. When it blares *EHHN! EHHN! EHHN!* he hits the snooze button, unbuttons the top button of his kitty-paw-print pajamas, and plummets back to sleep.

Benkle dreams. He's with his gorgeous, tall boyfriend, who is as kind as his toffee-colored face looks. Alfounz has sharp features, a strong, stubbled jaw, and muscles that bulge at rest. His long black hair cascades over his shoulders and the satin sheets.

He's quite a contrast to Benkle, who crawls over Alfounz's body, kissing his abs, his chest. Benkle's face is clean shaven, pale. His hair is just barely retreating from his original hairline. His nose is bold, on an otherwise soft face. Not for lack of trying. Alfounz reaches up, drags a finger along Benkle's eight-pack, and bites his lip in anticipation. He breathes, and his lungs quiver.

Their bed is flying around the base of Fae's World Tree, slowly spiraling toward the canopy. The Red Nebula fills the void of space and changes colors in different sections of the clouds to the beat of *Sex Coil,* by Brance Heldinger and the Finger Lickers, all while Monric—the Halfworld cityscape —the planet they orbit, Primordo, and the sun dance in the sky around them. The air above Fae's heart-shaped leaves comes to life with the universe's single most spectacular display of fireworks. Benkle and Alfounz embrace, and things get . . . blurry.

The shrillest song Benkle can stand wakes him from his slumber, and he instinctively reaches for his phone. Benkle tries to sound cheery, as he is happy to hear from his lover, but his sleeping vocal cords croak his boyfriend's name instead. "Alfounz."

"I need to get laid," Alfounz says in a voice with natural, sensual rasp. "Are you up for a quickie before . . . Wait, are you still in bed?"

Benkle sits up, blinking rapidly with max half-open eyes before he rubs the sleep out of them and says, "I think so." He throws his comforter off himself and walks up to his bedroom window and his ficus, holding his phone to his ear.

"You better get a move on," Alfounz says, "or else take a sick day, love." Light reflects off the skypiercer tower next door, through the windows of the skypiercer tower Benkle lives in.

"Mmmhmm." Benkle picks up the water pitcher to refill it and looks down to see that it's already full of water. The ficus is leafless, dead. "Fuck you, Huck." Benkle's knuckles turn white around the pitcher's handle. He puts it down.

"Your plants?" Alfounz asks.

"Yeah," Benkle says, wiping his face. He turns away from his dead ficus and stretches his free arm, yawning as he walks out of the bedroom.

Alfounz says, "If you'd given me a key, I could have watered them for you."

Benkle turns on the speaker phone, puts the phone on the counter, and says, "I know" while glaring at his phone. He pulls his water flosser off the counter and starts cleaning his teeth.

"And," Alfounz goes on, "if we just moved in together, we could save on so many expenses."

"I ah ah"—Benkle pulls the water flosser out

of his mouth and spits—"I am not anywhere near ready to move in together. My husband and I were together for three years. We've been together for three months."

A long silence is filled with the rush of water between Benkle's teeth. His bathroom is green tiled, from forest green on the floor to aqua on the ceiling. It has a glass shower eight feet in diameter, a marble squat toilet, and peach curtains over the three-foot-wide window. Alfounz says, "It's been five months. You've spent a lot of time as a string of tachyons recently."

Benkle spits. "What?"

"Teleporting."

"Oh." Benkle regards his face and looks at his phone. There is some need, but no time for makeup.

"I know you're living paycheck to paycheck again," Alfounz says.

"How do you know that?" Benkle asks, putting his water flosser down and picking up his phone to carry it back into his bedroom. He opens a door. An array of blue suits and brown kitten pajamas hang in the closet. Three blue top hats rest on the shelf above. Benkle considers wearing one for just a moment, like he does every morning, but he doesn't have the time to decide that he doesn't have the confidence to pull it off. He reaches into the closet.

"You're always more . . . generous when you have money," Alfounz says.

"Well," Benkle says, pulling out a suit and inspecting it, "maybe I just don't like you as much as I used to. Maybe I've traded up."

Alfounz laughs. "I'll believe you've traded up when I find porn on your phone that doesn't involve people who look exactly like me, but a little older."

Benkle tosses the suit onto the bed. "I'm seeing your father," he says.

"Ha!" Alfounz says. "Now there's someone who needs to get laid."

Benkle grins, and regards the top hats for a moment. He grabs one and tosses it on the bed. "I also have every porn Lip Heldinger has ever been in."

"Who doesn't?"

Benkle drops trou, revealing vantablack boxer briefs and very pale chicken legs. He's picking up his suit pants off his bed when his phone makes the noise of a cowbell. It's Huck, texting *What's the password on this computer again?*

Benkle rolls his eyes and tells his boyfriend, "Hold up. Huck's asking me another stupid question."

"I'm beginning to think," Alfounz says, "that those are the only kind he can think of."

Benkle says, "A-yup!" and types *Scroll up.*

Benkle presses a button on the rectangular base attached to the tiny madman's flute that is the key to his apartment. Beep beep! Click. His front door locks. Carrying his black briefcase and his top hat in the same hand, Benkle briskly strides toward a row of elevators just down a maroon-painted hall with dark-yellow-and-purple trim. His right pants pocket bulges with a BrilliantEats brand knock-off Nutty Bar, and his left pocket holds his gun.

A neighbor in an ill-fitting white space suit stares at the steel elevator doors and taps his foot on the linoleum. He holds his helmet in one arm and raises the other to look at his wrist. His golden-brown hair is styled like a handlebar mustache on his forehead, while the rest of his scalp and face are bare, teal skin.

"Hey, Khen," Benkle says.

Khen draws a phasor pistol out of his helmet and waves it at Benkle, paranoia filling his eyes. He sways on his feet like a bad dancer, or someone who's never heard of a firing stance.

Benkle draws his own phasor pistol from his left pocket, aligns his feet with the target to minimize his own target size, and points his gun right at Khen's forehead mustache. Benkle's phasor is fae green, his favorite color, with a silver-tipped barrel.

It has a little black speaker on the back, like all mon-modern phasors, that produces a tone. The law requiring them states that they let blind users know when their weapons have been fired.

"How's it going, neighbor?" Khen asks. He steadies his weapon on Benkle.

Benkle sighs. "Boss called me in the middle of the night, so now I'm running late."

"Always so negative," Khen says. "I bet that's why I never see you with anybody."

"I'll have you know," Benkle says, steadying his aim at Khen's mouth, "my boyfriend is hot, and I'm a workaholic."

"Sure. Sure." Khen grins jovially. He lowers his weapon, and Benkle points his own at the floor. The elevator dings, and Khen fires wild. The phasor produces a deeply satisfying tone. It turns an oval section of the steel elevator door next to Benkle's head into a liquid that glows red hot and drips down the elevator.

Benkle dives through the doors as they open. He picks himself up and scrambles to the elevator's buttons to press any one he can, and then jams on the close door button over and over again, crouched, phasor pistol at the ready, until the steel barrier moves between Benkle and the man who lives down the hall.

Khen says, "See you later, neighbor" through the holes in the doors before the elevator begins to move down. Benkle can finally breathe and search for the right button to bring him to the parking garage.

The sky is half Red Nebula, half black, flecked with stars. Xol, a yellow dwarf star, illuminates the cityscape from just above its horizon of skypiercer towers. A not-too-distant blue star sits along the red horizon. Benkle pats his temple with foundation while the autopilot of his fae-green econoluxury hovercar flies toward the electroshielded express entrance of Solscapes Interstellar Realty.

HONK! Benkle's autopilot automatically bursts with radio waves, warning Dr. K.'s homemade dumpstercar that it is invading Benkle's vehicle's personal space as she cuts Benkle off, nicking the side of the rectangular entrance on her way through the electroshielding. Benkle's hovercar brakes. The momentum jars Benkle, who gets foundation in his eye. "What the shart!"

Dr. K. double parks, taking her space and the only available unlabeled parking spot. By the way Dr. K. waddle-runs for the door, it would seem she really has to pee. Benkle watches her, flat faced, while he slips his foundation into the glove compartment.

At the front of the garage, Huck's cherry-red Gosh Quasar-T is also double parked, taking up Benkle's spot. Benkle throws his hands up, saying, "What the shit!?" Benkle has to hover back outside and down the building, pay the toll, go through a lower garage, pay the garage fee, and ride the elevator up. He looks at his phone. It will take an hour—if he's *really* lucky.

Two hours later, Benkle finally leaves the elevator and huffs as he marches toward Mrs. Lotterydale's office, carrying just his black briefcase. Snarling, he rubs his head, wishing he'd worn his top hat.

Standing in his way like a six-foot-tall wall, Huck might have been handsome once, but if that was ever the case, it certainly was no longer so. Huck has a white-knuckled grip on his own briefcase, the mythral box. He's shaved today, and he recently, rapidly went from paunchy to slightly emaciated, hairy to androgynous. His mop of hair has been chopped down to what looks like a fairly stylish lesbian cut. Whatever face that overprivileged idiot wears, he's ugly to Benkle.

"I've been waiting for you," Huck says. "You're late."

"I know," Benkle says, scowling. "I'm sorry. It won't happen again."

"You better make sure that it doesn't," Huck says.

"You better learn to park your damn car, and get the Huck out of my way so I can get our itinerary from your mother."

"What?" Huck asks.

"Nothing," Benkle says. "Just get out of my way."

"I feel like something just happened there that maybe I should be concerned about."

A faint clicking sound like claws on tile comes from down the hall.

Benkle asks, "What is that noise?"

A cartoon—Huck's elecre—steps out of the board room. It turns its purple, dragon-like head toward Benkle, runs up, leaps and tackles him.

On his back with a ninety-pound elecre slobbering all over his face, Benkle asks, "What's Poyo doing here?"

Huck holds the briefcase and a finger up, saying, "Hold on. I'm on the phone. Yup. Yup."

Poyo licks all of Benkle's foundation off his face.

"Yup." Huck shakes his head. "Nope." He nods. Huck raises his voice in anger. "Well, same to you!" He ends the call with a click and puts the phone in his brown pants pocket. "What were you saying?" Huck asks.

Benkle pushes the electron creature's massive head out of his way to speak, but Huck starts again. "Turns out it's cheaper to use the tolls than it is to pay for high-electron gruel five times a day, plus Poyo destroys my apartment when it doesn't get enough attention."

Benkle stands up, and Poyo rubs against him, wagging its tail and smiling with that giant hell mouth it has.

Huck kneels down and pats Poyo on its thick neck. He puts on an infantile voice to say, "It's almost naptime, isn't it?" He lowers his tone and turns his face toward Benkle: "Come to our office. I need you to take down a letter for me."

Benkle straightens his shirt and asks, "Can I go get your briefing from your mother?"

"I got the briefing," Huck says. His pace picks up, no doubt stimulated artificially. "It's all good. We're going to space today! Technically, we're skipping space and going to another planet, like we do every day! And the journey will feel instantaneous, but it will take weeks, most likely."

Benkle lets the tense side of his mouth relax just enough to ask, "Which planet?"

"Secret Planet!" Huck says.

"You are," Benkle says, "without a doubt"—he starts walking past Huck—"my least favorite person."

Huck swings the briefcase and says, "I'd fire you if mother would let me. So, about that letter."

"Fine." Benkle pulls out his phone.

Huck dictates: "Dear Infernal Council, It would appear that you flaming ducks do not understand the gravitas of the situation. My mother—"

"I have to stop you there." Benkle holds his phone down and gestures toward Huck with his middle finger. "A) Never mention your mother if you ever want to be taken seriously." Benkle adds his index finger to the mix. "B) Duck is a post-autocorrect word, unless you mean the bird, which . . ."

Huck shakes his head, so Benkle goes on: "Then its closest translation in Infernal is not something you want to call an entire organization that could kill you in the most agonizing way possible just by touching you. And C)." Benkle raises three fingers at Huck. "What was C)? Oh yeah, it's the Infernal Fucking Council!"

As they approach the stairway and a chute marked "Confidential Fire," Huck says, with an entirely unearned air of confidence, "Let me worry about the politics."

Benkle's eyes droop. "Your mother told me to never let you anywhere near the politics after that fiasco at the auction."

They walk in silence for a moment with their anger at each other facing forward, because neither of them wants to look at the other. Huck goes for the door handle to the stairwell, but Benkle steps ahead of him and plants himself in front of the door.

"Give me the plan sheet," Benkle says.

"I got it," Huck says. He pulls a wrinkled screenpaper out of his blazer pocket, balls it up, and throws it into the chute marked "Confidential Fire."

"Ooh," Huck says. "It's hot in there. So many secrets."

Benkle crosses his arms. "Why are you in such a mood?" he asks.

Huck opens his eyes very wide and says, "I may have developed a coke habit."

"No shit," Benkle says.

"YES shit," Huck says, reaching past Benkle for the door handle. "That shit is expensive."

"Well," Benkle asks, stepping out of the way, "what are we doing?"

Huck opens the door and says into the stairwell, "It's need to know."

"No it isn't," Benkle says, standing in the threshold of the door, holding it open while Huck starts down the stairs.

"Yes it might be, for all you know," Huck says with a grin.

"I'm going to talk to your mother."

"Ha!" Huck says. "You lose, sucka. She isn't here."

Benkle instinctively reaches for his gun, and pauses, considering his options. A breeze moving through the stairway into the hall lightly wafts both men's hair. The soft sounds of footsteps down the stairs and conversational voices are followed by a laugh. The inaudible conversation ends, but the footsteps grow louder. "I shouldn't," Benkle says under his breath. "I need the money."

"What was that?" Huck asks as footsteps approach from below.

Four people walk up the stairs toward them. Dr. K., a blond woman in a ponytail with bottle cap glasses, one lens concave and one convex, is in her red jumpsuit. She is accompanied up the stairs by two extraordinarily unremarkable engineers dressed in the same jumpsuit, and Jomic, a bold-mustached man in a tiger-orange suit and a top hat with a brown patch sewn onto it.

"Okay," Benkle says. "You win." He lets the door shut behind him and follows Huck down the stairs. "How am I supposed to assist you if I don't know what we're doing?"

Jomic looks over at Dr. K. and says, "But, as far as we know, there is no rhyme or reason to it. It's like they were all arbitrarily designed by a variety of different—"

"Ha!" Huck shouts at Benkle. "I won!" The president turns down the stairs toward the newcomers, waving the briefcase at them. "You all just saw him . . . with your ears." Everyone pauses. "Get your sorry asses back to work!"

The whole group raise their eyebrows at Huck, and they squeeze past him and Benkle on the stairway.

Benkle looks down at Huck from a few steps

up. "We should get to work, too, whatever that is."

The shrillest song Benkle can stand comes from his phone, which Benkle realizes is still in his hand. The text says *I've got something special planned for your birthday tomorrow.*

Huck rubs his ears and says, "Good point. Follow me," and leads Benkle down the stairs.

Ooooh, Benkle types, stepping carefully down the steps—at least for someone who isn't watching where he's going. *I can't wait to see what's in store for me.*

The door into the hall opens before Huck and Benkle get to it. The new guy steps into the stairwell, a devastatingly handsome man with slick black hair in a pink suit and a long, brick-colored tie. Huck puts a hand on the door and watches the new guy hurry past them up the stairs.

Benkle sees what he believes to be a tinge of lust in Huck's eyes, and he's immediately forced to choke down his gag reflex.

CHAPTER 2:
A REWARD FOR THE RETURN OF BISH-HOP OF IHS

Huck types away at one holomonitor while Benkle sits in a folding chair on the other side of the table, shaking his head at him. Benkle turns around in his seat and asks Ègwen, "Why did you come back to work for Solscapes?"

"Came back?" Ègwen says, standing in the threshold between Benkle's newly charred, formerly blue office and the hall. The door is stopped against the wall to let the air pull out the remaining smell of burnt plastic since the air vents were melted, then froze in an all-but-useless lump. "What do you mean?"

Huck types away at the computer at the cheap plastic folding table he shares with Benkle as a desk. The mythral box rests on the floor to Huck's side. Poyo sleeps next to him in its eighty-pound purple-dragon form, snoring softly.

"I heard you left," Benkle says, "but then you were here the next day."

"I don't remember quitting," Ègwen says. "Who'd you hear that from?"

Benkle says, "Dr. K."

Ègwen purses her lips to the side thoughtfully.

Benkle asks, "Do *you* know what Huck and I are doing today? Huck's death grip on the mythral box earlier tells me we're probably getting mythral from somewhere, but his lips are tighter than his puckered butthole."

Ègwen cringes and says, "No, sorry."

On top of the table Benkle and Huck share as a desk is a file, sitting open. The screenpaper on top says:

> *Bish-hop of Ihs*
> *Upper limit 323 sexvigintillion*
> *Realtor: Ferele Miden*
> *1182974736 Tarder Street*
> *Metrofidelis*
> *Godslands, Dragonthrone*

The page is full of text, information that Benkle glances over with glazing eyes. Benkle shakes his head and asks Ègwen, "Does this job make you as suicidal as it makes me?"

Ègwen frowns at Benkle and says, "It makes me more homicidal." She steps up to Benkle and puts her hand on his shoulder. She asks, "Do you need anything?"

"I'm not actually suicidal." Benkle slides his eyes to the side to side-eye his boss. "I just hate Huck."

After a moment, as Huck keeps typing, Ègwen glances in his direction and says, "Me, too."

Huck stops typing and asks, "What was that?"

"We hate you," Benkle says.

"Oh." Huck proceeds with his typing.

Ègwen shakes her head and says, "You really shouldn't joke about suicide."

"What?" Benkle asks.

"You said the job makes you suicidal. I hope you weren't trying to be funny."

"Sorry, Ègwen," Benkle says. "I wasn't trying to be funny. It's just an expression."

"A problematic expression," Egwen says, pursing her lips again.

Huck suddenly stops typing and presses a button on the base of the holomonitor, shutting the hologram off. While Ègwen and Benkle watch, he stands up, knocking his chair down onto its back. Poyo stirs slightly, opening a single eye, and then it's right back to snoring. Huck stops to pick up the chair and put it right before he walks up to the door. Ègwen steps to the side. Huck says, "I'll be right back."

Benkle says, "You know, Ègwen, I think

you're the only Employee Resources Director I've ever known who isn't a rat."

"Thanks," Ègwen says, smiling as she leans against the door.

The new guy appears in the open threshold. He's devastatingly, overwhelmingly handsome. His black hair is short and stylish. His pink suit has a white pocket square and he's wearing a white button-down shirt. His brick-colored tie matches his o-ring knot belt. He looks around the room, raising his eyebrows, holding a large screenpaper in his hand. The paper has lines and curves and numbers and names on it, and a cartoon cloud with a lightning bolt. It's a map.

"I was told to bring this to Mr. Lotterydale," Ren says.

"Oh. Hey, Ren," Ègwen says, stepping away from the door. She waves hello.

"Hey, Ègwen." Ren says.

Benkle resists the urge to rub his eye and says, "I'll take that."

Ren says, "I was told to give it to Mr. Lotterydale." He pulls the map up against his stomach. "Where is he?"

"I don't know," Benkle says.

"When is he going to be back?" Ren asks.

Benkle leans back in his folding chair. "He just left, didn't say where he was going, but said he'd be right back."

Benkle asks the new guy, "What do you know

about the plan?"

"What plan?" Ren says.

"Whatever Huck and I are doing today," Benkle says.

"Well," Ren says, "there's a map involved, and I was to take it from a filing cabinet and give it to Mr. Lotterydale."

"Can you tell me what the map is of?" Benkle steps up and tries to get a closer look at the over-sized screenpaper.

Ren shrinks away from Benkle, pulling the map up against his chest.

Benkle groans, takes his seat, and pulls out his phone. He presses a button, and illustration of a simple chart with a red arrow bursting from the top, to check his stocks. The numbers are red, in the high quintillions. If only he'd bought mythral when it was cheap. He scrolls down, and an article shows the current mythral numbers, 95 novemtrigintil-lion. As he watches, it drops about 50 decillion credits per second. The arrow on the chart show-ing the day's return points straight down. "Fuck! I'm going to choke whoever convinced me it's better late than never!"

Ègwen shakes her head.

Benkle brings up a holo of the news on his phone, and the praying mantis announcer says, "This is for the stock advice," and she eats her co-host's head. Benkle turns off the news.

Benkle turns to ask Ren, "Did anything pan

out with Cinema Maximum?"

Ren turns to face Benkle and says, "I interviewed, but I couldn't do it. I think that every color of magic has its own taint."

Benkle shakes his head, and his glabella wrinkles. "That's . . . That's awful. Look, maybe I took the wrong approach last time we spoke."

"Yeah, you did."

"And *maybe* I kind of deserved that shiner you gave me."

"Yeah, you did."

Benkle says, "I just want to let you know that I have no hard feelings."

Ren says, "Do you have any idea what it's like to be able to cast all nine types of magic? Not that I ever cast any of the white magic, obviously. For a few brief years I was on my way to the top of the world, and now I see things, not only the ghost of my brother, but I see myself riding emotional waves. I get depressed in a way that never happened before. I can tell that I've lost some amount of compassion. It's like my soul is just as corrupted as my mind."

Benkle sits back in his chair and crosses his arms.

Ren says, "It's like—to some extent—the symptoms seem to balance each other out a little bit, but that only helps to mask how bad it really is."

Benkle rubs his eye. "You just have to rub it in that you're a Spectrum Wizard, don't you, you conceited dickhole."

"What the fuck is your problem?" Ren asks. "Do you want another black eye?"

Benkle stands up, and he goes for his gun.

"Whoa!" Ègwen shouts. "What's going on here?"

"It's okay, Ègwen, " Benkle says. He takes his hand away from his pocket, without his gun. "Can we have a minute?"

Ègwen looks Benkle over, then she looks Ren up and down. "Okay." She steps out the door.

Benkle steps up to the new guy. "Look, Ren, I'm sorry. What you described, that's not my experience with wizard sickness at all. I don't know for sure that this is it, but I find myself significantly less able to control the words coming out of my mouth."

Silence washes over the room. Ren turns his face away. Benkle rubs his eye.

"So you haven't always been this insulting?" Ren asks.

"Only since I started working for Mr. Lotterydale . . . and the worlds' wizards started going insane."

"A likely excuse," Ren says. "I'll be right back." He turns and walks out the door. He stops and waves the map as he says, "Don't let Huck go anywhere if he comes back."

"He's not smart enough to listen to me!" Benkle shouts.

Huck returns, saying, "We're off to Elysium!"

"Oh, really?" Benkle says. "That's not nearly as awful as I expected. I'm still going to be a string of tachyons on my birthday, but whatever."

"Old wizards are retiring in droves, so the tolls alone *should* be worth enough to let us buy back the tower. No, wait. We're going to Kew first. The century-long realty boom seems to somehow be buffered against the corruption of magic . . . I think."

"So," Benkle asks, "which is it?"

Huck breathes oddly heavily and says, "I guess you're just going to have to find out."

Benkle sighs and scrolls on his phone. "I'm getting paid overtime for every day I spend as a tachyon, so whatever."

Huck clears his throat.

"Actually." Benkle puts his phone down and says, "I have a suggestion for you."

Huck tells him, "Proceed."

Benkle says, "I think you need to stop playing mind games." Huck sits down on the chair across from Benkle. "You're not very good at them." Huck nods. "And you shouldn't be playing them with your staff. That's something you restrict to your family."

Huck makes a quiet "Mhmmm."

"They are a lot less likely to sue you."

"Ahh. Yes," Huck says.

"So," Benkle says, "that's my suggestion."

Ren steps in through the doorway.

Huck stands up, straightens his blazer, bends over the desk to get real close, and gives him the bird. He puts the bird right up in his face, pressing against his squishy nose.

Benkle catches Ren chuckling and looking at Huck's bent-over buttocks. Benkle swallows, and then he gapes.

Huck ponders Benkle's disgusted expression for a moment before he looks over his shoulder at Ren. He stands up and straightens his blazer. He winks at Benkle, who shudders in response. Huck turns to face the newcomer.

"Wait," Ren says, getting a closer look at Huck. "Is this . . . ?" He looks down to Benkle, who nods. "Oh. You're Mr. Lotterydale."

"Huck," he says, extending his hand.

Huck and Ren make a long, painful amount of eye contact. Their eyebrows move up and down and sideways while their hands clasp and their eyes explore each other's bodies.

Benkle dry heaves.

The pair stop gawking at each other and gawk at Benkle.

Benkle says, "I love myself too much to subject myself to that. That *would* make me suicidal. I want to live, *and* enjoy life. When you're ready to tell me what the fuck we're doing today, I'll be in my office."

"My mother burned down your office," Huck says. "It's where we are right now, in case you forgot. It does look a lot different in here."

"I did forget!" Benkle says in a higher than usual pitch. "I'll be in the break room!"

Benkle escapes. Huck sits down and gestures, offering Ren Benkle's seat across the table. Huck looks up from his folding chair and asks Ren, "Why . . . How long have you worked for Solscapes?"

"About a month and a half, I think," Ren says, taking the other seat.

"What an asshole," Huck says, looking at the doorway where Benkle just left.

"Oh my god," Ren says, nodding emphatically.

Huck opens his mouth. They sit, looking at each other for a moment. Huck closes his mouth. Words don't come to either of them. Ren opens his mouth. Each of them has questions. Ren closes his mouth. Neither is really prepared for the answers.

"Well ..." Huck sighs. "I should go grab that little bastard from the break room. We probably should have left a while ago. I'll see you around, Ren."

Mrs. Lotterydale rides in the back of her hoverlimo, into a tower on the Central Bulge, a vaguely nipple-like mound of terrain and cityscape collected at the center of Monric's flat eastern hemisphere.

Mrs. Lotterydale almost forgets her mask, but her limo pilot reminds her with a honk of the horn, waving the fly mask by its proboscis out the window. Fluffy antennae, like long, black-and-gray feathers, extend from the top of the mask, which is covered in gray fur. Mrs. Lotterydale's hair is down, even whiter than her skin. She wears gray robes with a brown streak running across the top, sending tendrils down the length of them; evenly distributed between the tendrils are tiny black and white spots. Her shoulders are covered in the same gray fur as her mask, both fashioned after the psychodidae, or drain fly.

She hurries through large, empty adamantium corridors, adjusting her mask.

Past a couple armed guards and through an ornately carved stone door, Mrs. Lotterydale finds a room barely large enough to hold a small oval table, and five people sitting around it, most in black, each wearing a different fly mask. Blackout curtains run the length of one wall. Floating orbs near the ceiling light the room a little dimly.

A feminine voice is muffled by a mask with orange eyes and two gold stripes around one black. "Welcome, Psychodidae. Where is Fruit?"

"He had some business I needed him to attend to, Flesh, so I'll share anything pertinent with him." Mrs. Lotterydale takes her seat next to a tall member in a crane-fly mask.

A sort of masculine, nasally voice comes through a mosquito mask. "I think we should get started. We're late enough already."

"Well, then," the largest of the seated says. "It looks like the alliance with Caramoore's Claws has been approved."

"I'm sorry to interrupt, Lady Hero," someone says. They're wearing a mask that's almost all eyes and proboscis. "I think there's a more pressing matter at hand."

"If it's important enough to interrupt me over, it must be pretty important. Proceed, Snipe."

Snipe picks up a small, white plastic clicker and clicks it, and a life-like hologram appears above the center of the table. The holo recording takes place between two two-story, brown stucco buildings with red doors, facing each other. The watery world called Stonis is low on the horizon, and Gravita encompasses most of the visible sky while the Red Nebula takes up the rest. In the foreground, a primitive cityscape is burning. A scream comes from the hologram, and rapid footsteps.

A small crowd of people step into the hologram and stop, dumbfounded, shocked, and awed.

A black dragon flies overhead, and it's followed by a white dragon. The white dragon opens its mouth and fires an invisible stream of liquid hydrogen at the black, whose backside freezes solid. The black dragon plummets toward the ground, unable to stretch its wings. In mid-drop, the black dragon's entire body bursts into flames. It thaws and catches itself, dragging its flaming tail across rooftops at its lowest point.

By the time the fiery dragon reaches the white, it's already engaged in a spiraling dance of death with a horned, bearded daemondragon. Its furry bat wings claw as ferociously as its fore- and hind limbs. The fiery dragon inhales, and exhales death as its flames turn blue and a jet of white-hot breath bursts from its mouth in a tempest, burning the daemonic and snow dragons to the bone. Their bodies—minus the scales and the soft tissues of their heads—fall to the ground, and the crowd at the forefront of the hologram collectively sigh in relief. "Thank the Fates!" one shouts. Another raises a fist in victory.

The black dragon lets its flames die out, turns, and flies back the way it came.

Snipe presses on the clicker, and the holovideo pauses. "The unusual part here, for those of you that don't know about dragon culture, is that the whites and the daemons were fighting each other. They have been like this"—Snipe crosses his fingers—"allies for as long as anyone can remember."

Mosquito asks, "Why should we care about dragon culture?"

"It's a possible portent for things to come," Snipe says. "The really interesting thing is just about to start." With another click, the video resumes. A tall, muscular, barrel-chested, naked man opens the door to the building on the right.

"What's this here?" the naked man says under his breath, stepping out to look over the primitive cityscape, genitals gently wafting in the breeze. A fireball rises from a burning building in the distance. The man cocks his head at it, mumbling to himself. He sticks his finger in his own asshole, pulls it out, and examines his finger with his eyes. Then he examines it with his mouth. While sucking on his shit digit, he waves his other hand, and the gawking and gagging onlookers grab their heads and fall over screaming while blood drains from their every orifice, their skin turns pale, and the light fades from their eyes.

"Is there a point to all this?" Lady Hero asks.

Snipe says, "The point is that the corruption of magic is at least as far as Elementus."

Mrs. Lotterydale says, "I told you that months ago!"

Snipe says, "Well, if you did, Psychodidae, I didn't trust you enough to write it down or even commit it to memory." Snipe raises the remote. With a click, the holo changes, and the shit licker is replaced with a fully clothed man; a caped business warrior appears with his hands on his hips, rotating in the hologram. "And here we see one Bish-hop of Ihs, aka Bish-hop of Metrofidelis, aka The Big Turkey King. He's the owner and CEO of Middle Management Incorporated, and he's been missing for two months."

Bish-hop's clean-shaven, peach-skinned chin is held high. His broad shoulders are under some sort of light-gray, metal-elemental-hide vest and matching cape, worn over a button-down spandex tunic, high dress in his homeland of Ihs. Around his neck the Ihsish CEO wears a series of progressively longer but smaller-gemmed gold and ruby necklaces, hanging almost to his navel. He wears rows of gold stud earrings, and numerous sizable gold-and-ruby rings prevent him from fully closing his fists. Each ruby is etched with a different intricate rune.

His outfit is topped off with a simple looped crown of gold, adorned with a single white crystal. A no-doubt-powerful rune is etched into the center of the crown, which is resting securely on his gray-templed head.

"If anyone has any information," Snipe says, "please come to me with it. Here's my card"—Snipe passes out paper rectangles, tossing them across the table—"in case anyone lost my number." Snipe taps on the table three times: ba-dum bum. "Otherwise, the Bish family assassin has left an outstanding threat against my testicles."

"Why are they threatening you?" Mosquito asks.

"I don't know. I only just met Bish-hop when he stayed at one of my hotels, before he went to Solscapes to look for some property to buy."

Snipe straightens in his chair. He says, "The assassin said the Bish family said that Bish-hop put explosives in all their heads and a sensor in his own heart. They said if he dies, they all die, and then my testicles die. So we know he wasn't dead as of this morning."

Mrs. Lotterydale says, "Signal transfer from interstellar objects can take years."

"Oh"—Snipe's vocal pace increases, and his tone hardens—"well, regardless, they're not going to let my testicles live if I don't find Bish-hop."

Mrs. Lotterydale says, "While I'm sorry for your loss, I don't see what our society can do for you in this instance."

"YOU LOST HIM!" Snipe accuses, pointing a black-gloved finger at her.

Mrs. Lotterydale cocks her masked head in contemplation and says, "No I didn't."

The whole group speaks at once, from outrage to laughter at the lie.

Snipe says, "What the shit?"

Mosquito says, "You definitely did."

Flesh says, "Liar."

Lady Hero chuckles.

"Oh, come on," Mrs. Lotterydale says. "My realty wizard went insane and stranded him goddess knows where. You all saw the video!"

"Some excuse," Snipe says.

"YOU made us watch the video!"

The tall, skinny woman in a skinny crane-fly mask—otherwise silent up til now—leans over and whispers to Mrs. Lotterydale, "Don't pay attention to them, they've all lost their skull sponges." Her voice box might be as old as Mrs. Lotterydale's.

Snipe stands up, putting his hands to the table, and he says, "I think Solscapes, as both the entity responsible for the disappearance of Bishhop"—Mrs. Lotterydale huffs and crosses her arms—"and the best equipped to search as a realtor, should scour the star cluster for any sign of Bishhop of Ihs and for any places that may not be affected by the corruption of magic." Snipe takes his seat.

"What?" Mrs. Lotterydale asks. "You do realize I can't do that."

Lady Hero stands up and says, "You must."

"Whatever you say, Lady Hero." Mrs. Lotterydale strains to control herself for her superior.

Crane announces, "I'll put a few credits down for the effort, and I suggest we all do the same. We all have a vested interest in this."

"Thank you, Crane," Mrs. Lotterydale says. "With enough money and our com crystals, it should be easy enough to discover the breadth of the corruption."

"So," Mrs. Lotterydale says, putting her hands on the table, "I can take hard credits, or give you my accountant's digits."

"I don't think that's going to happen," Snipe says.

Crane speaks up: "Psychodidae needs resources to cover her expenses. She's not as rich as she was two months ago, and she was the least of us then."

Mrs. Lotterydale slowly turns her fly-masked head to stare at Crane.

"It is for that reason," Lady Hero says, "Psychodidae must prove herself worthy of this esteemed council. I forbid anyone from aiding her financially in this matter."

Mrs. Lotterydale throws her hands down on the table and shouts, "What!? This is going to bankrupt us!" Mrs. Lotterydale leaps to her feet.

"Find a way," Lady Hero says.

"DUCK!"

"Sorry, Betsy," Crane says, shrugging.

Mrs. Lotterydale turns to her wordlessly, pleading with her palms up. Crane turns away, and Mrs. Lotterydale directs her gestures around the table. Everyone folds their arms and looks away, except Lady Hero and Snipe.

"If that concludes this item, we have a substantial number of them on the docket today," Lady

Hero says. "Our merger with Caramoore's Claws should substantially improve our standings, so the first priority, I think, is tithing increases."

"With that, we can increase the funds going toward insider information and ponzi research and technology." Most everyone around the room nods in approval, except Mrs. Lotterydale.

Flesh rubs her gloved hands together and asks, "How much of an increase are we talking about?"

Lady Hero gestures toward Snipe.

Snipe says, "One tredecillion should be plenty."

The group bangs their gloved fists on the table, signifying all-but-unanimous approval.

"I quit," Mrs. Lotterydale says.

The crowd falls to a hush.

Mrs. Lotterydale says, "It's obvious that you're railroading me, scapegoating me for things you know are outside of all of our control. I'm done. Armies of the rich be damned. I'm going to go enjoy my last years, or whatever."

Flesh says, "Good luck trying to enjoy it without any money."

Mrs. Lotterydale says, "Maybe I'll just keep casting red magic until the wizard sickness kills me. That could be fun."

Crane stands up and puts her hands on the table before her. "Look." Her voice is stern. "Nobody here likes the Lotterydales."

Mrs. Lotterydale slowly turns her head toward Crane, considering a red spell.

"But we need the Lotterydales," Crane says. "Their com crystals and teleportal may be this council's only link to the worlds outside this solar system." She stands up and walks toward the window. "With the corruption of magic, instant interstellar communication has become prohibitively expensive. Indeed, Solscapes may be the only thing that keeps the Fly Society intact through the next few years, because I don't know if you've looked outside, but things are not getting better."

Crane pulls back the drapes, and Fae is in full view. One of its leaves is on fire.

In the foreground, worker androids in hardhats are pushing against the collapse of the skypiercer tower next to them. Their propulsors light up in blue streaks from their palms and soles. It's as if a clean cut was sliced through the buildings at a thirty-five-degree angle, fifty floors from the graduated, diamond-shaped top. Four androids carry the ends of metal cables and use them to apply even pressure along one side of the loose upper floors of the building. Another android solders the cut, re-attaching the broken top of the building to its base. The androids who were holding the building up fly away toward other disasters.

"I have a teleportal," Snipe says.

"Yes," Crane agrees, "but have you had any success finding mythral so you could duplicate it?"

"No," Snipe says, lowering his head.

"Meanwhile, Psychodidae here"—Crane points a long arm, palm up, at Mrs. Lotterydale —"has two fully functioning teleportals."

"And a mythral box," Mrs. Lotterydale says. "I had to do things even I feel shame about to get it."

"I didn't think you could feel shame," Crane says.

"Neither did I!"

A disk-shaped hovercraft wobbles in the space between the buildings, and crashes into one of the androids holding the lower cable. The android is squished between the slightly dented hovercar and the damaged building. The orange cat sitting in the driver's seat shakes their head, takes a drink from a large green bottle, and drives away like nothing happened. With this, the androids on the upper cable have to compensate. They overcompensate; the top of the building tips, and they push it over the other edge. It plummets more than a thousand stories. The androids carrying the cable look at each other, and one shrugs before they fly off toward another disaster.

"And the search for a place free from the corruption ..." Crane closes the curtains. "That could save our very souls."

"Alright," Flesh says, "maybe we should help Psychodidae instead of throwing her to the wolves."

Lady Hero knocks on the table in agreement.

In a moment, the whole table is knocking, except Snipe, who crosses his arms, and in a tone that conveys his eye rolling despite his mask, he says, "Fine."

CHAPTER 3: DESTINATION UNTOWARD

Huck looks up from the map and walks away from a massive, looming glacier through a dense forest. The frozen tele-portal they came from stands against the glacier. A pine ent toll guard shakes its trunk at the pair of realtors, slack-jawed and furrow-browed. Clouds race toward the frozen lands as Huck and Benkle step off the snow onto crispy, semi-frozen leaves.

Huck holds the edge of the map in one hand and supports the bulk of it on the back of his other hand, which is clinched around a briefcase. Poyo, gliding just overhead, has pink cartoon scales on its belly. It yawns with gaping jaws and instantly transforms into a floating eel-pillow.

The red sun stays at the horizon. Long coronal loops threaten to flare at any moment. This certainly isn't Elysium, and Benkle imagines that it probably isn't Kew either while glaring at Huck's back. Stepping downhill, Huck glances up from the map at a sudden coronal mass ejection, and he asks Benkle, "Are you going to quit on me?"

"No," Benkle says. "I'm not going to quit on you. I need to eat. But I do need you to stop being such an asshole."

"What?" Huck asks. "Why are you calling me an asshole?"

"Well," Benkle says, "you still blame me for the gravity pool."

Huck steps on a round, flat-topped rock and says, "Because that's your fault." Poyo, in its eel-pillow form, glides through the air toward Huck's back.

Benkle glares at Huck. "Where are we going?" he asks.

Poyo closes its eel-pillow eyes and bites onto the back of Huck's collar.

Huck says, "I'm not sure yet. I'm only good at thinking on my feet, so I'll figure out where we're going while we walk." The terrain is uneven, with roots and fallen trees and mossy deathtraps. Huck's foot falls into one. If it was deeper than a couple inches, it could have sucked.

Benkle follows Huck and the snoring eel-pillow around a large pine tree and says, "No one ever accused you of being good at thinking in any situation." Secretly, Benkle admires the way Huck can navigate the forest floor, while Benkle stubs his toes and narrowly catches himself. He stops for a moment, hand on a tree that Huck narrowly didn't walk into, wondering *How is he so uncoordinated in every other situation?*

"That's not true," Huck says. Poyo's pillowy tail sways in the slight breeze, like a white ponytail. "In algebra 2.3, another kid said I was the dumbest smart person he'd ever met. I still remember it as one of the best compliments I ever got."

Benkle nods, saying in a high pitch, "I can see that!" He looks down and drops his voice. "I'm sorry. I can't seem to control my mouth anymore."

"What are you apologizing for?" Huck asks, squinting at the map.

Benkle opens his mouth to speak and closes it again.

Huck says, "I wrote a story over the coke-fueled weekend. Well . . . it's kind of the first chapter of a story, but I hope it will stand alone. Right now I'm calling it 'A Song of Dick and Fart Jokes.' What do you think of the title?"

Benkle's upper lip curls unintentionally.

There's a rustling behind them, high in the trees. A denim-clad individual with dark skin and a short, conical hat flies over the canopy, laughing manically.

"Was that Ferele?" Benkle asks.

Huck stares into his map and says, "She's flying toward the stream!"

"Yeah," Benkle says, looking at a ten-foot-tall, trickling waterfall, and the creek running glacier to sun side a few hundred yards in front of them. "I can see that." He rushes past Huck, who folds the map in half and trundles alongside Benkle. Somehow, Huck is a fraction as agile as when he's got a screen in his face. Huck falls and catches himself on a root.

Benkle stops to wait for his boss to pick himself up while he gawks.

Huck clumsily rushes up to Benkle and asks, "So, do you think she's still using magic?"

"I don't have words to express how stupid that question is." Benkle shakes his head, turns toward the river, and runs. "Just come along."

"So we can warn her?" Huck asks.

"YES . . . IDIOT! FUCKING GECK! I HATE YOU!" Benkle picks up speed, and his foot catches on a root. Benkle goes down.

"Wow," Huck says, standing over Benkle. "Tell me how you really feel."

Benkle picks his head up off the forest floor and wipes dirt off his face, mostly smearing it. "You could make things a little less unnecessarily difficult."

Huck raises his hand as if it was in a sock puppet and mimics Benkle: "You could make things a little less unnecessarily difficult."

"You fucking—" Benkle puts his dirty fingers into the space between his eyes. "We need to find Ferele, so how about we both just shut our cockgobblers and figure out how to cross this stream?"

"We could step over it," Huck says, "or at least

I can. Maybe I could toss you across."

Benkle's lower lip juts out, and he reaches into his pocket for his gun.

Manic laughter upstream sounds overhead, and the denim-clad wizard flies above them toward the tributary, and turns in the sky to follow the creek downstream.

Huck says, "That's definitely Ferele."

Following the flow of water and the fading laughter, "oohs," and the occasional breaking branch, Benkle and Huck hop from rock to stream-rounded rock. Purple passion flowers climb short rocks, folded closed wherever the sun breaks through the canopy. Huck has the map in one hand and the briefcase in the other. Benkle steps on a foot-wide, light-tan stone just like ninety percent of the other tan stones, but this one folds in with Benkle's weight; its spine snaps, and its intestines shoot three feet out of its butt.

Benkle stops to stare at the carnage he caused with a single step. "Oh my gods." He steps back and dips his shoe in the water.

"Worry about that later," Huck says, shuffling along the stony path. A dozen rocks just like the one

Benkle broke under his foot stir and rise an inch or three from their places in and around the stream. They raise hairy whiskers and fleshy claws. "Shit!" Huck yells. "*Fishcrabs!*"

Benkle hops over one fishcrab. It looks up at him with its flat, whiskered face. The fishcrab rotates on its spiny *leg fins* and nips at him with a long, fleshy *claw fin*. It clips a hole in Benkle's sock. "Ouch!" he yelps and picks up the pace.

They round a bend in the stream where it cuts through the hill like a luke-warm knife. The short gray cliff face is sheer, with sparse vines winding up from the fertile soil next to the stream, to the trees growing from the cliff's edge. Downstream a hundred yards or so there is another tributary, and the collective flow of water goes from stream to larger stream, or maybe river.

Ferele stands by the Maybe River looking down at her foot. She wiggles that leg and stomps on the ground with the other foot. Behind her, creeping up as silent as a mouse, is sixty feet of yellow-and-brown snake, a Galalosi python.

Ferele struggles against her stuck foot. She shakes her leg. She bends over to pull on her shoe while the snake slithers closer.

Benkle hollers, "Look out, Ferele!" but the distance between them and the water rushing past them dampens his voice. Benkle steps hesitantly onto another round, tan rock, and then less hesitantly, and then he runs toward her.

Huck says, "Are we sure we want to run *towards* that snake?" An eighty-foot Galosi python slithers out of the forest a few dozen feet behind him. Huck yelps and scurries after Benkle.

The snake behind Ferele rears up, its jaw unhinged. Ferele gestures at her boot like she's having a conversation with it, pleading with it not to do this to her again.

Huck's foot lands heavily on a rock, and the rock's intestines shoot out of its butt into the whiskered face of another rock. The rocks all around them stir, their claws chitter, and they inch toward the offworlders. Huck's eyes dart around, landing on the snake, which is easily keeping pace behind them, and he scampers after Benkle.

Benkle shouts, "Look out, Ferele!" but the snake is already pouncing. In one moment, Ferele is arguing with her stuck boot, and in the next, the snake surrounds her, swallowing her whole.

"Oh shit! Oh shit! Oh shit!" Benkle whispers. "Fuck!" He puts a hand up to stop Huck and grab onto something, anything. He pulls his fistful of Huck's blazer and everything attached to it close to him, and whispers, "We're too late!"

Huck is a little paler than usual. He opens his mouth, but no words come out. He looks over his shoulder, back the way they came.

"Do you hear me?" Benkle asks, still in an urgent whisper. "Ferele's dead!" He never takes his eyes off the snake that just made a meal of Ferele. It turns its head side to side, as if looking for another meal.

Huck grabs Benkle by the shoulders. Huck swallows and opens his mouth. His terrified eyes lead Benkle toward the snake behind them, narrowing in on its targets. Benkle turns his fully opened eyes back at the snake across the river. It's reared up again, looking directly at them.

Benkle draws his phasor pistol. "Ow!" Benkle yells as a fishcrab pinches his ankle. With a deeply satisfying tone, the phasor fires into the critter's back, burning a hole straight through to the soil. A swarm of fishcrabs surrounds them. Benkle raises his gun toward the larger of the snakes. A fishcrab leaps from the ground and latches itself to Benkle's face. Benkle drops his weapon and claws at the creature attacking him.

Benkle pulls the little creature off his face, only to see the giant creatures cornering them. One makes a wiggling bridge out of its own body, crossing the river. The other slowly approaches, watching them, sizing up the challenge of fighting these little people without the element of surprise. It doesn't seem to think that challenge would be too great.

The fishcrabs nip at their feet with their claws. Huck backs into the cliff. His eyes veritably glow at the sight of the vines. "This way!" he says, throwing the briefcase up over the rocky wall. He reaches up for a vine and takes it in his hand. He pulls himself up about an inch, and the vine comes off—detached from the face of the cliff.

Huck grabs another vine and pulls. It comes loose.

Benkle says, "Climb the rock, you idiot." He reaches up for a rough lip of rock, and securely takes a hold. He pulls himself up about three inches, and the rock comes off the face of the cliff. It slides harmlessly down, but Benkle has to start from square one while the snakes slither up to striking distance. They obviously know each other, because they move in tandem, cutting off their prey's escape routes with the length of their tails.

Huck tugs at the pillowy eel swaying in the breeze, attached to the back of his collar. "We could use some help, Poyo!" Poyo snores slightly louder, but its eyes don't open.

Benkle finds a hold and pulls. He finds another, and another. Huck finds a hold and climbs up after. Benkle reaches the top, not far enough above to deter the snakes, but maybe enough to give them a running start. He reaches down for Huck's hand as a snake coils up at the bottom of the cliff and strikes from below.

Huck takes Benkle's hand and claws at the top of the cliff with the other, dislodging a large rock, which tumbles right into the attacking snake. The snake collapses. The rock rolls off its caved-in head, and its sphincter releases the foul-smelling matter of its last, half-digested meal. The other snake regards it, unhinging its jaw, and then it wraps its mouth around the head of the other snake.

Benkle and Huck waste only a few moments in awe of the cannibalistic giant and the horde of fishcrabs gathering to fight each other over the big snake's last shit, before the realtors flee for dear life.

Benkle and Huck reach a lake and stop to catch their breath. The red sun hasn't moved from the horizon in millions of years. Across the lake sits a town made of cedar and stone. The Maybe River empties into the lake a few hundred feet to their right. Across the lake, a two-story cedar building and an empty one-boat dock sit at the outskirts of the town. A pea-gravel road leads back toward whatever civilization this is. Benkle doesn't know because that asshole Huck won't tell him.

"The map's not getting a GPS signal," Huck whines. "There's no red dot signifying where we are."

Benkle takes a deep breath and asks, "Do you mind if I see it?" Benkle braces for the inevitable petulance.

"Here," Huck says. He hands the map over

to Benkle, who looks up at him, dumbfounded for a moment before he reaches for it, fully expecting Huck to withdraw it at the last moment. Benkle snatches the map and side eyes Huck. He unfolds the large screenpaper and asks, "And where are we going?" The upper-left-hand corner of the map is labeled "Diadox."

"L Town Twee," Huck says.

Benkle nods, looking down at the map, and says, "We should follow the shoreline." He turns left and steps along the shore. He folds the map in two and holds it to his side. "I can't believe that we just watched Ferele die."

Huck shudders and asks, "Was that bigger snake eating the less bigger snake?"

Benkle says, "Yes."

"So she's inside a giant snake inside an even gianter snake."

"What's your point?" Benkle turns to stop in front of Huck and look him in the eye.

"It's just . . ." A rustling in the treetops distracts Huck for a moment. He keeps staring. ". . . a good way to go."

"What is wrong with you?" Benkle asks, and before Huck can answer, breaking branches and manic laughter precede the airborne appearance of Ferele, flying out of the woods and over the lake. "Oh shit!" Benkle shouts.

Ferele descends across the lake. She makes a skillful landing on the empty dock, and proceeds to walk to the building. Benkle and Huck turn around and run along the shore toward the Maybe River delta. It's almost definitely a river. Benkle unfolds the map. "It will take us a good hour, but we can circumvent the lake. We've got to do it anyway to get into town."

"I say we wade the river," Huck says with coke-fueled arrogance and a hand on his hip. A tiny, five-pound iceberg drifts down the river, into the lake, from the nearby glacier.

"That water looks cold as shit," Benkle says. "I'm not going in it."

"Shit is generally warm," Huck says, putting down his briefcase. He rolls up the sleeves of his blazer.

"It's an expression," Benkle says.

"I guess cold-blooded animals would probably have ambient-temperature shits, wouldn't they?" Huck rerolls one of his sleeves. Sleeping Poyo drifts in the breeze.

Benkle says, "I wouldn't know. I'm not a zooscatologist."

"Really?" Huck exclaims in what seems to be genuine surprise. "What is your degree in, then?"

Benkle huffs.

"What?" Huck asks.

"Fuck you."

"No," Huck says. "I'm really asking."

Benkle eyes Huck for a moment before he says, "Liberal arts."

"Oh," Huck says, "I guess that makes sense. Well, Benkle . . . What's your last name?"

"Cherryblossom."

Huck stops messing with his half-rolled-up sleeve while he eyes Benkle. "Really?

"It's Faeish."

"Well, Benkle Cherryblossom, AA, I think—"

"I have a masters," Benkle says. Ferele walks out from behind the building, back toward the dock.

"Really?" Huck asks. "I didn't know they gave those out for liberal arts."

Ferele pulls something out of her denim suit pocket and kneels down over the dock.

"Oh, no!" Huck says. "I think she's casting a spell!" He stops fucking with his sleeve, which is now mostly unrolled, and grabs the briefcase off the ground. "I'll wade the river! It's not that big."

Huck steps into the water with Poyo still attached to his collar. "Oh shit! This is cold as shit!" He takes a deep breath and another step into the water. A shard of ice breaks on Huck's ankle. The current rips him off his feet, and Huck and the briefcase are each sent in separate directions into the lake. Poyo bobs, partially in the water, still attached to Huck's collar.

Benkle crosses his arms and shakes his head at his boss.

CHAPTER 4: ATTACK OF THE PENIS MONSTER

"I really didn't want to do this," Ègwen says into her phone, "but I'm forced to have a conversation with Hedra." She walks down the magenta hall. Her puff-ball hair is in a fluffy ponytail with the sides hanging out. She wears a sheath dress with black and white polka dots in layers on top of each other. A big white spot covered in black spots is on her shoulder. A big black one covered in white ones is on her opposite hip, under her misty-teal-colored belt.

"What?" she asks. "Yeah. I'm at his office now . . . See ya."

As she puts her phone away, she gets an obnoxious notification. Ègwen's phone says, "Emergency Alert! Solar storm warning. Communications may be disabled for an indefinite period today."

"Hmm." Ègwen shakes her head and puts her phone away. She raises her fist at the door marked

"Dr. Hedra Nalyaci, WFC," over the words "Vice President of Casting."

A tall, purple dragonmade suddenly appears in her periphery. "AHH!!" Ègwen shouts. She looks up at the monster in a white apron and mushroom hat. "Oh, Ormr." Ègwen takes a deep breath. "You are impossibly light on your feet."

"I think it's this floor." Ormr raises a booted hind claw and drops it on the stained tile. The thump is muted. "Benkle nearly made me shart myself in his adorable little kitten jammies last month the exact same way."

Ègwen nods, pursing her lips to the side.

"I wanted to know," Ormr says, "if you're coming to game night tonight, so I know how much food to bring."

"I am," Ègwen says.

"Good," Ormr says, stepping past Ègwen and down the hall. "Make sure you bring plenty of money."

"I will," Ègwen says, grinning.

She turns to face the door, then sees where she is, and her grin sours. Ègwen raises her fist and knocks on Hedra's office door. The knock pushes it open. The knob hangs loose. A couple feet from the corner of Hedra's office, a brain lies on the floor. "What the . . ." The door swings open, revealing a body lying on the other side of the floor, face down, still, breathless. It's a pale, bald man in deep-dark-purple robes.

Èíwen stands on the threshold and stares, unable to move or even understand what she's seeing. A holographic screensaver, an unnecessary relic of early monitor technology, plays above Hedra's desk. A holographic chihuahua puppy rolls over, stands up, pants, lies down, and appears to go to sleep. Eventually the holomonitor's light fades to nothing as the computer goes to sleep, leaving the whole office dim. The reflections off nearby hovering traffic out the window spread chaotic flashes of light across parts of the room.

A little man steps up behind Èíwen. The gnome looks around her and says, "Oh shit!"

Èíwen turns her wide eyes on the gnome in his well-fitted black suit. "This isn't one of your practical jokes, is it, Cotl?"

"I wish I'd thought of something like this," Cotl says, "but no. This is more like something I'd pull on my brother, or my mother. At work . . . This is almost as bad as a glitter bomb."

Cotl steps into the room and kneels over the body. He puts his fingers up to the carotid artery and confirms: "This is no joke. They're dead . . . and I think it's Bort."

"Oh no!" Èíwen says. Her eyebrows furrow, and she tears up instantly. "And what happened to his beautiful hair?"

Cotl stands up straight and locks eyes with Èíwen. "Did Hedra finally do it? Did he kill him?"

Èíwen pulls her phone from her pocket and

presses the call button. Nothing. "That's right," she says, "the solar storm. My phone isn't connecting to anything. Yours?"

Cotl pulls out his phone and glances at it. The phone's cover depicts a black-and-white t-square fractal. "No."

Ègwen turns to run but stops herself long enough to say, "Wait here. Don't let anyone in or out." Then she's off.

Cotl shouts after her, "I'm an expensive guard!"

Ègwen hollers back over her shoulder. "That is not my problem!"

Three voices yelling in an r-heavy extraterrestrial language follow Ferele as she steps out of the wrong building. The door closes behind her, and the noise is replaced by the sound of the Maybe River flowing and sea bats chirping and diving for fish in the lake. Ferele asks herself, "Why do people always shout at other people that they know don't speak their language?" She looks east to the edge of the ball of red fire that is this world's red dwarf star, where it's locked to the horizon. The forests to either side are dense and hilly, leading toward the glacier that feeds the Maybe River, opposite the ever-setting sun.

Ferele lets the door close behind her, walks off the pebble path, and kneels over a patch of dirt on this otherwise-lush stretch of landscape to pick up a small stick. A few scrappy blades of grass grow, but the soil is so light and poor that nothing else will. She whistles a tune while she drags the stick through the dirt. The tune is half-composed of two different but adjacent tracks on Ferele's baby-niece's favorite album, and half-made out of a song Ferele no longer remembers the name of, or more than ten notes of, but has been whistling and humming for decades. It could be from an old TV commercial or the theme music for a circus.

Ferele raises her stick from the dirt and turns her head up, saying, "I should probably be getting ready to go to work or something." She looks back down at her spell circle for a moment. Spirals and sharp lines and simple mystic symbols surround the central point. Closest to Ferele, there's a fairly large, empty circle within the larger circle, surrounded by its own mystic symbols. "Soon," Ferele says. She puts her palm down on the empty circle within the spell circle, and as the dirt is smoothed out by the magic, erasing the spell circle, Ferele is elevated from the ground.

The effect only lasts for a moment as she gently falls back the few inches she rose. Ferele stands up straight and jumps twenty feet into the air. "What was I doing here again?" she asks herself, hovering where she leapt. "Was I looking for something?" She sighs. "I'll think while I fly."

Ferele soars a little higher above the canopy this time, avoiding the stray branches reaching into the sky that she doesn't see while cloud gazing or staring at the ground directly below her. Too high and she might get caught in the rapidly moving wind overhead, or attract unwanted attention.

Ferele circles back. "I remember what I was looking for! A gift shop!" She waves her arms and summons a digital map of Northeastern Diadox on a large screenpaper. The display zooms in on the narrow path of habitability that loops around the sun-facing side of the world. "Ferele, you'd be lost without magic."

Ferele releases the map and the magic that summoned it to her, puts her arms up, then pulls them back down, seemingly pushing herself higher into the air. As she rises above the town to try and find the shopping district, a flailing figure in the middle of the lake draws her attention. She turns in the air and descends slowly, cautiously.

As she recognizes who it is, she cocks her head and arches an eyebrow at Huck Lotterydale, one of her boss's bosses. He's clean shaven, and his hair is shorter than normal, but the red blazer is a giveaway.

Ferele gently glides down to levitate just over Huck, a foot above the water. Huck splashes frantically, struggling against the pull of gravity and the crabs swarming around and on him. Ferele asks, "Do you need some assistance?"

With a surreal sensation, Ègwen steps up to Mrs. Lotterydale's office door slowly. Mrs. Lotterydale laughs behind the glass door. Her ombre for today is milk chocolate and pink. A walrus in a yellow suit and top hat sitting across from her desk laughs with her, and Flora, Mrs. Lotterydale's Stonisi assistant, looks up from her clipboard at the door.

Flora mouths the word "curtain," and the light passing through the glass door begins to fade into the magenta of the hall while Mrs. Lotterydale glances at the door. The walrus turns around to look over his shoulder and through a monocle at her for just a second, until they all become shadowy magenta outlines of themselves and fade away entirely as the door takes on the appearance of the wall. A spark of electricity runs up and down it, and the door reverts back to clear.

Ègwen reaches for the handle, but apprehension stays her hand. Flora steps between the irate-looking pair and the door and opens it.

"She's in a meeting," Flora says. She closes the door behind her. "What do you need?"

Ègwen asks, "Is your phone down?"

Flora nods. "What's the issue?"

"Bort is dead."

"What!?" Flora's eyes and mouth open with shock and grief.

"Bort is—"

"Oh my . . . Did Hedra kill him?"

"That's what Cotl and I suspect," Ègwen says. "Cotl's watching over the scene, making sure nobody contaminates it. Are the com crystals affected by the solar storm?"

"I don't know," Flora says. "They all go specifically to different planets anyway, or wherever their paired crystals are. You couldn't call the police with them."

Flora turns to share a concerned glance with Mrs. Lotterydale and says, "Quarantine the area, send Cotl to see me, and make sure nobody but the police gets into Hedra's office."

Benkle shouts across the water, "Don't do it!" but Ferele doesn't seem to hear him over the splashing and the wind. She pulls a pulp-paper notepad out of her pocket and a fine-pointed pen. "Don't cast any magic!" Benkle yells. "It's tainted!" His stomach gurgles. "Lordy. I should eat my Nutty Bar soon."

There's a rustling sound in the woods. Benkle turns slowly. He reaches into his left pocket to find it empty. His gun is somewhere along the Maybe River. A small branch reaching from the shadows rustles, and Benkle dismisses it. Probably a small, harmless animal.

Benkle calls out again, "Hey, Ferele!" but she never stops drawing her spell on her notepad.

The rustling in the shadows intensifies, and as Benkle turns to face it, a two-hundred-pound, peach-colored insect steps into the light. Benkle turns to flee the four-eyed creature with wide, sharp mandibles and what could only be described as a thick-haired peach mustache, unless this were a lighter situation, at which point any number of comparisons could be invited, such as an archway of tiny dicks or a mustache of pink penises.

Benkle drops the map as he runs and reaches for the nearest tree branch. He heaves himself into the tree. The creature's body is long, not unphallic, with its head resting just in front of all six of its legs, and two six-inch penis-like structures wiggling from its ass.

The creature steps up to the tree and turns its head up. Benkle stands on a thick lower branch and glares down at the beast, which turns and starts circling the tree.

"Fuck you, diving beetle," Benkle says, flipping it the bird, confident that this mostly aquatic creature would consider climbing for a meal that's almost its own size too much of a risk.

A chittering draws Benkle's attention toward a nest a few branches up. The two-hundred-pound diving beetle larva steps away from the tree. The chittering turns into an outright brawl between two of six baby squirrels. This draws the attention of the diving beetle. It reaches its hooked forelimb up to the lowest branch and tests the limb for stability. Benkle climbs higher in the tree, toward the nest.

Inside the nest, four of the baby squirrels turn their massive black eyes on Benkle while two of them circle each other, chittering furiously. Benkle reaches into his right pocket. This one has what he seeks inside. He pulls out a BrilliantEats brand Nutty Bar, peels the purple wrapper, and breaks the nutty treat up over the squirrels' nest. The bickering siblings stop to sample the sticky substance filling their nest with a decadent nutty aroma.

With two legs on the branch, and a third reaching up, but no chittering luring it toward an easier meal than the arboreally agile—comparatively, at least—Benkle, the the diving beetle larva pushes off from the branch and turns to investigate a rustling in the woods.

Benkle's stomach gurgles, and the beast turns around. It circles the tree, presumably looking for an easier way up.

Rustling in the underbrush, a Galalosi python slithers up behind the beast. The diving beetle freezes for just a moment before it suddenly switches into rapid fire. Its legs move jerkily. It reaches for the lowest branch. Its foreclaws hook into it. It starts climbing the tree, fleeing from the python slithering up behind it.

Benkle climbs upward and out, away from the trunk onto a precarious branch, while the beast climbs the branches closest to the trunk, and the snake coils around the base onto the lowest branch.

Benkle quietly begs the beast, "Don't climb onto this branch! Don't climb onto this branch!"

The snake wraps itself around the tree and coils its way up. The beast backs away from the snake, onto Benkle's branch.

The branch dips, and Benkle approaches the ground. The snake's head turns toward Benkle, and it slithers toward the dipping branch. The snake's eyes widen from their slits, taking in all the light they can before it strikes.

Benkle backs farther away, to an even more precarious position on the branch. It bends and dips with the weight of both Benkle and the giant insect.

Benkle tears his eyes away from the monsters in front of him, to the ground below him. It is probably the most immediate threat. If he falls and hurts himself, he'll be helpless. *It's not too far down,* he says to himself.

Without warning, the baby squirrels leap out of their nest, directly into the face of the diving beetle. Their rodent teeth cut through its antennae like they are unshelled walnuts. Four of them go for the eyes.

Writhing and wiping at its face, the giant insect jerks on the branch Benkle clings to.

The branch sways up and down, and Benkle is forced to hang on for dear life, digging his nails into the wood, as the giant snake approaches from below, abandoning the diving beetle larva and the climb, for now, in favor of this human who will likely soon fall out of the tree.

The beast falls onto the snake, squirming and scratching at its eyes, cracking the ribs underneath it as it lands. The snake turns to strike at the beast and latches onto it with its fangs, catching an eyeful of squirrels itself. Within moments the blind, bleeding beast runs southeast while the broken, blind snake slithers southwest.

Benkle climbs down the tree, reaching the bottom as the baby squirrels, as adorable as ever, reach the foot of the tree and start the climb up. "Thank you," Benkle says, then he blinks, his brow furrows, and he shakes his head before he steps away, approaching the shore. There, he sees Ferele still drawing on her notepad and Huck still flailing in the water.

Benkle puts his hands up to his mouth to

form an amplifier and hollers at Ferele again. She turns her head to look at him.

Ferele puts her finger on the spell circle on her notepad, and Huck rises from the water, along with a few scaley, feathery, biting critters.

"OW!" Benkle hollers. A walnut falls next to him after bouncing off his noggin. Above him, in the squirrel's nest, the mother is chittering at him furiously. She picks up another nut and tosses it at Benkle's head.

CHAPTER 5: CRAB KINDS AND ROCK MIMICS

Ègwen sits in a folding chair next to the door, legs crossed, refreshing her *Sosocial* app over and over and over again. A breeze comes down the hall, ruffling her little hairs and making them stand on end. The breeze opens the door an inch, and the rust on the hinges creaks. She reaches over to pull the door closed and rererefreshes her Sosocial app.

Ègwen hears a noise on the other side of the door. She turns to look behind her and sees Reine the myrmidon coming down the hall. Their stick carapace is covered in ants and wearing a pleather suit.

"What's going on?" Reine asks.

Ègwen opens her mouth, and closes it. She puts her phone in her pocket. She raises her hand, palm up, pursing her lips, and then drops her hand.

She uncrosses her legs. "Not much," she says, patting her thighs.

"This is why I like playing cards with you," Reine says. "What's really going on?"

Ègwen opens her mouth, but nothing comes to her until she finally says, "Bort's on this side of the room," gesturing across and behind the door, "and . . ." She points her thumb behind her, toward the brain on the floor behind the wall. "He's dead."

"Oh no . . ." The myrmidon's wooden face mimics the appearance of human concern. "Are you alright? I know we don't know each other well, but I know you and Bort had a special relationship. Hell, I think everyone around here had only the best to say about him, and I'm not just saying that because he's dead. Do you need anything?" Reine pulls their head back, curiosity getting the better of the queen ant inside the colony inside the myrmidon. "Why are you here instead of the police?"

Ègwen crosses her legs again. "That's nice of you to ask, the second question, I mean, but unless you can get the solar storm to go back up the sun's butthole—sorry. The phones aren't working, so we can't call the police."

"Oh . . ."

Ègwen cocks her head at Reine. "Is there something you wanted to talk to me about?"

"Yeah, it just seems like a bad time." Reine steps past Ègwen. "I'll catch up to you soon."

"What is it?" Ègwen asks. "I could use a distraction."

Reine stops and turns around. "Almost half my advisors have said they want us to quit."

Ègwen purses her lips and narrows her eyes at Reine. "I'm not sure what you mean."

"The advisor ants in here with me in this head," Reine says, while knocking on their wooden skull with their wooden knuckles.

"Oh . . ." Ègwen says. "The best I think I can do to help with that is give you your paperwork, when you're sure."

The myrmidon purses their wooden lips. "You don't understand. I agree with those advisors, and none of them advised *against* quitting."

"So," Ègwen asks, "you want me to help you quit right now?"

"Three-sevenths of my advisors say, 'Yes.'"

"O . . . kay," Ègwen says. "I can't really go any- where, though. If you ask Jam, she can give you all the paperwork you need."

"Oh . . ." Reine says with a thoughtful expres- sion. "Okay. Thanks."

"You are still coming to game nights, though, right?" Ègwen asks.

"Of course," Reine says. "It's the highlight of my week. Last week, when Dr. K. tried to bet one of the engineers, I found that quite amusing. And Ben- kle's stories about President Lotterydale's incompe- tence have all been written into my library." Reine points at their head.

"Oh," Ègwen says. "You wouldn't be willing to read me those stories, would you?"

"We'll get the game night group together at a bar sometime, and I'll give you all the highlights."

An ogre in a black t-shirt and jeans comes down the hall. He has white earbuds in, and a red, swollen, bruised thumb. A breeze whips through the corridor and pushes the door into Hedra's office open.

Reine steps away, but stops, glancing up at the towering green monster approaching them, who's mouthing the words to the song he's listening to as he walk-dances down the hall. Reine turns back to Ègwen and says, "Don't let the ogre see." They glance at the door. Ègwen follows their look and sees that the breeze left it ajar. "He's got a really squeamish stomach. He'd probably projectile vomit just at the thought."

Ègwen takes the handle of the door, and it comes right off in her hand, and the door slips open further. She turns to Reine for advice, but they are already walking down the hall. Ègwen slips into the room and behind the door to push it closed. The ogre's footsteps crescendo as he approaches.

Ègwen shouts, "You can't come in right now, sir! There's been an emergency!" The footsteps stop. Something else stirs inside the room. Ègwen steps back and looks around the office. The lights are off, so only the reflection off the neighboring towers and local traffic illuminates the room, to erratically varying degrees. Dark shadows fill two of the corners.

A single knock at the door sends it open wide.

The ogre blinks at the unexpectedly swinging door, seeing the missing handle just then, and looks down at Ègwen. "Oh . . . Hey." He holds his injured playing thumb up, pulls his earbud out with his other hand, and looks around the room. "I'm here to see—ŌGH!" The ogre projectile vomits at the sight of the brain, all the way across the room and onto it.

With a flick of the wrist, Ferele releases her telekinesis spell and drops a soaking wet Huck Lotterydale onto his ass on the rocky shore, next to a shallow stream, where it falls down a twenty-foot cliff face into a pool that itself drains into the lake. Ferele glides gently to the ground.

"You saved me from those"—Huck coughs up a little lake water and spits it out—"from those . . . Those weren't fishcrabs."

"*Dinocrabs*," Ferele says.

"Dinocrabs?" Huck asks.

"Yup."

Huck whips some of the water off his sleeve

and says, "I'm surprised it's not colder this close to the glacier."

Ferele says, "We're a quarter of the way to Sunside."

Huck cocks his head. "Wow." He glances over to the shoreline. "How many kinds of crabs are there?"

"Let's see." Ferele puts her hand up to her chin and looks up into the sky at a rock-colored monster flying above the forest across the lake. "I've seen hermit crabs and squat lobsters, true crabs, false crabs, like *fishcrabs* and dinocrabs, various *mammalcrabs*, like *pandacrabs*—they're super cute—*turtlecrabs, lizardcrabs*. It must be good to be a crab. *Birdcrabs*."

Huck sniffs and says, "I meant, like a number, not a list."

"Of course!" Ferele says.

Huck reaches for the back of his neck and finds nothing attached to his collar. He looks around. "Have you seen Poyo?"

"Oh, Poyo's here?"

A lurching pink-and- purple cartoon creature crawls out of the water, chomping down on a dinocrab. Huck runs over to hug his elecre friend. "I should have figured you'd be okay." Kneeling, with his arm around Poyo's thick neck, he turns his head up to say to Ferele, "Do you have any idea how late you are for work?"

Ferele squints and grits her teeth. "Too late to

see if this town has any neat gift shops?"

Huck nods, eyes wide.

Ferele nods complacently, then she notices something. "You shaved your beard."

"I did." Huck narrows his eyes at Ferele. "Guess how late you are."

"Well, let's see . . ." Ferele looks to the sky while she ponders. "I have no idea."

"Take a guess," Huck says.

A breeze ripples through the leaves, and the forest grows quiet. The water is still and clear.

Ferele says, "Fifteen . . . minutes?"

Huck bursts into laughter.

Ferele grins nervously. "How far off was I?"

Huck says, "I have no idea."

"Hey," Ferele says, "you want to go see if this town has a gift shop?"

Huck says, "I'd love to, but we both have work to do."

"I'm sorry." Ferele explains: "I haven't been myself lately. Easily distracted. On top of the world one minute, so sad the next."

Huck grimaces. "About that . . ."

Benkle uses the lake as a mirror and splashes

water onto the mud on his face. "Huck is going to get me killed," he says. He glances over his shoulder, into the forest. "Either he or his mother. What the fuck is going on with the animals here?"

He kneels over the map, which is covered in mud and sand fleas. He looks at the water, considering washing the screenpaper off.

"I shouldn't," he says out loud. "I have no idea if this is waterproof." He shakes the screenpaper, spraying the water with mud. He wipes it off with the side of his palm, and an eensy little flea, heavily laden with fertilized eggs, leaps off the mud, up under the cuff of Benkle's shirt.

A rustling in the forest freezes Benkle. His head turns suddenly, and he reaches into his pocket to find it empty. A chipmunk walks out of the forest and sits down, looking up at Benkle.

After a few seconds, Benkle breathes, and he moves again along the shoreline. He avoids the rocks that are too round. He stops to look at one that's a little less flat topped than the ones he knows are dangerous, but he doesn't contemplate it long; he needs to keep moving.

So, Benkle opens the map and trips. He picks himself and the map up and scowls at himself. He's now dirtier than before he washed his face in the lake. He wipes off his face while glancing side to side, then examines the map. The lake is only half a mile wide. He should be able to find Huck and Ferele without too much trouble. Should.

The shore is covered in round rocks that all look suspicious to Benkle. He opts to step into the woods and avoid this stretch of the shore. "They have to be right in front of me. And if they're not, I'll just head back to the teleportal."

A burrow in the ground gives Benkle pause, and he lengthens his roundabout path by a few more yards.

A shadow crosses over Benkle, and he looks up to see a large flying creature. Benkle assumes this monster is less comfortable to live inside of, and freezes, praying silently that it doesn't see him or want to eat him.

The creature turns in the sky. Its gray color makes it look like stone. It seems to be a descendant of a tetrapod, based on the appearance of its limbs, but there are six of them, and its wings are more like a dragonfly's, while its head is entirely alien, mostly tentacles and tusks. With the creature circling above Benkle, the slightly built executive assistant can only assume he's been sighted and targeted.

Benkle sprints into the woods, and the monster dives toward him. He dives into the burrow.

The myrmidon brings a bucket and an electromop to Ègwen, who's seated just outside Hedra's office.

"Thanks," Ègwen says. She takes the bucket of water and puts it on the floor. She takes the electromop from Reine and puts the mechanical-tentacled end in the bucket. "How did you . . . ?"

"I heard it happening from down the hall," Reine says. "I'd have gotten you the janitor instead, but she is dealing with an issue in Dr. K.'s lab."

"He," Ègwen says. Reine cocks their head at Ègwen quizzically. "The janitor uses masculine pronouns, or at least doesn't correct anyone when they use them to my knowledge."

"I do not understand pronouns," Reine says. "I wish humans used hierarchy-based pronouns like my species. It's a lot more intuitive."

"In a way," Ègwen says, "they kind of are hierarchy based."

Reine raises a wooden eyebrow. The breeze kicks the door open again, and the aura of the vomit wafts over them. Reine puts their hand over their nose and says, "I'll see you tomorrow about the separation paperwork. Jam is just . . . She scares me sometimes, you know what I'm talking about?"

Ègwen swallows away her desire to gag. "Yeah," she says. "She scares me every time. I'll see you tomorrow." Ègwen frowns as she looks into the poorly lit room. The reflections off nearby hovercraft erratically alter the lighting. She takes the handle of the mop and drags the bucket across the floor, into the threshold.

Reine walks away, and Ègwen mops away. The mop just pushes the stuff around. The vomit simply seems to expand, never coming up. Ègwen rubs and scrubs and dabs, all to no avail. She burps, covering her mouth. "It is *so* gross in here."

A gurgle startles Ègwen. It came from inside the room. She peers into the shadows, the large black void under Hedra's desk, the corner behind the inexplicably exposed brain, which lights up as a delivery vehicle passes in front of the window. The boxy hovertruck says "Elecre Worlds are Better Worlds," over an array of all the most popular electron creatures. Ègwen pushes the door open wide and examines the other penumbras in the room from afar.

Ègwen's blood pressure rises until she can hear her own heartbeat. She steps deeper into the office and looks around. There are disk maps of the worlds of Elementus tacked to the wall, with Infernus slightly overlapping Gravita and Stonis. For some reason the Riverworld is next to Kvelt, the Elemental Plane of Ice, and smaller maps of the system's gas giants and water worlds. She almost believes she hears breathing.

She stands as still as she can, holding her own breath, listening. The door creaks as the breeze pushes it closed again.

"Hey, Ègwen!" Flora shouts from the door-way.

"Oh shit!" Ègwen shouts. She grabs a stapler off of Hedra's desk and raises it above her head.

"Wow!" Flora says. "I don't think I've ever heard you swear." She holds the door open, and her clipboard tight to her chest. "I don't think you should be in there. Oh my divine, what happened here? It smells like there's been a second murder, or like whoever made this vomit had eaten some shit."

The gurgling returns. Ègwen turns confidently toward a particularly dark shadow in a corner. She inches forward.

Flora says, "I need some paperwork for an incident with the teleportal. Apparently, this one doesn't like solar storms."

Ègwen throws the stapler at the darkness. It hits the wall and falls to the floor. Ègwen turns to Flora. "I thought I heard someone in here."

Flora pulls the door partially closed and looks around it. "If Bort gets up, I'm sorry, but I'm leaving you for zombie food."

Ègwen says, "Keep describing what you smell."

Flora covers her nose and says, "It smells like a room full of diapers and bile."

Ègwen eyes the shadows as Flora speaks. Flora retches and closes the door between her and the foulness, opting to shout through the barrier instead.

"It smells like someone fed an anteater nothing but vieux boulogne cheese and thioacetone. It's like someone cut open a beached whale for its ambergris, then—"

Ègwen interrupts, "What the heck is ambergris?"

Flore says, "Gray amber."

"I'm still lost. Can I assume it stinks?"

"Yes," Flora says.

Ègwen says, "Proceed, then."

Flora continues. "Then the person cutting into the whale died inside the thing, a few months passed, and a pack of wild dogs ate the whale's last shit before they entered and diarrhea-ed all over the inside of the whale. Then they ate each other's shit, and shat the double processed shit. It smells like—"

A retching sound comes from underneath Hedra's desk. Ègwen turns toward it and balls her fists.

Benkle crawls out the other end of the hole, into darkness. He pulls out his phone and turns on the flashlight. He's standing in a small cavern, a couple yards wide. Shadows obscure the passage deeper in, but a wind coming from it leads Benkle to believe that there is probably another way out. He steps deeper into the darkness.

The walls of the cavern are streaked with pale-green ooze. "Why is it always green ooze? Never purple ooze," he says to himself out of nervousness. He walks toward the passage deeper in. "Actually, there are a lot of white and yellow oozes." Benkle suppresses his gag reflex.

Benkle tries to avoid the wall ooze as he follows the wind. At the narrow passage into the next cavern, a gust pulls the slime off the ceiling, right into Benkle's face. Benkle gags and wipes himself off.

Benkle raises his light and steps into the next cavern, where he sees a long worm with oversized eyes. It stops to look back at Benkle for a moment before it withdraws from a scurrying fishcrab. The fishcrab nips at the worm with its fleshy claws and skitters on modified spines. Its long whiskers rub on the wall as it chases the worm's tip, completely unaware that the length of the worm stretches across the floor of the cave a couple times underneath it.

Water trickles out of the wall to his left, feeding the ooze and flowing like a thin sheen over a quarter of the cavern floor. Dark earth lines the other wall, and sharp gray rocks litter the floor. Benkle picks up one of the rocks and throws it at the fishcrab. It hits. The critter squeaks and skitters off.

The worm looks at Benkle, and approaches. Benkle stares for a moment, watching the worm wiggle like it's doing a happy dance. This critter is certainly novel, and it gets a grin from Benkle.

Benkle walks through the cavern, and the worm follows. The worm moves from its cute-eyed end, and the end leading out of the room pulls away. The wind keeps flowing like a stream through the underground passage, pulling drops of ooze from the walls and ceiling and dropping them in a near-constant sprinkling.

Benkle wipes his face off again. *Breathing. The wind seems to be breathing. That's all it is. That and my echo maybe.* Benkle continues farther into the darkness, where the cavern gets cramped.

The light comes from above. One length of the worm's many rises straight up a short wall of rock, the only way through. The wall is slimy, but jagged rocks make for easy climbing, when Benkle doesn't pull them out and drop them on the worm. It shrinks away, and Benkle apologizes: "Sorry." But it happens four times before Benkle figures out which rocks are solid enough to hold onto while climbing. "Sorry . . . Sorry! . . . Oh my gods, I'm so sorry!"

At the top, there's a narrow ledge overlooking a vast emptiness. *Why are we even here?* Benkle asks himself. *Is Mrs. Lotterydale trying to get us killed?* Benkle's ears perk as a noise comes through the wind. *Was that breathing?* It was. *I really think it was.*

Just along the wall on Benkle's side of this cavern, there's a dim light coming through another passage, and more of the worm's length rapidly moving into the light. Benkle sighs. He puts his phone in his pocket and presses his body up against the wall, feeling every nook and bulge, every sharp edge and all the slime mold on the face of the rock as he pushes himself onward.

Am I ever going to make it out of this cave? Benkle asks himself. *If I die in here, is anyone ever going to find my body? Will my soul get lost? Oh shit. I think I'd rather die on Fae if given the choice, or at least with a view of it.*

The light of day comes through the top of the next cavern, thirty feet up, and water cascades down one side onto mounds of dark-gray hematite, to splash against forest-green lichens on the wall. The worm moves into the shallow pool that takes up half the cave, away from Benkle, at a surprising speed. The worm's head catches up to him, following the same path he had taken into this cavern. It squints and cocks its end to the side, giving Benkle the most adorable gesture a pink tube with eyes can, and slithers along the edge of the water. Light also comes through a small hole in the wall of the cavern.

The worm leads Benkle toward one of the gray mounds, half-covered in water falling from above, as it rests at the far end of the waterfall, half-dry, in close proximity to the wall. The mound is sloped enough, and the rock face just next to the waterfall has ridges Benkle could definitely climb.

As Benkle approaches the mound, it rises above the water, the upper jaw of a monster many times Benkle's size, a *cavernous anglerfish*. It truly has a cavernous maw. Its teeth are two feet long, straight rods haphazardly poking out of the monster's jaws. Its eyes open, beady objects a foot wide. The worm extends from its forehead, a part of the cavernous angler itself, retracted into a single thick worm. It rises up out of the water, thickening and shortening, until it becomes a stubby version of itself hanging from the cavernous angler's forehead. By the array of worms-lengths on the ground, Benkle has to assume there are more where that came from.

Benkle turns and flees, and the monster lurches forward.

A cute little bug-eyed worm wraps itself around Benkle's ankle. He falls hard onto the cavern floor.

Benkle kicks at the slimy assailant and claws at the wall of the cave to bring himself to his feet. Benkle stomps on the worm while the ugly, terrifying cavernous angler lunges at him.

Benkle's heart feels like it's about to give way as he skitters into the hole with the light coming out of it, just in time to spare one of his shoes from being eaten by this monster.

CHAPTER 6:
HOT
CHIHUAHUAS

Flora says, "It smells like someone used their personal yeast to bake a loaf, and then they cooked it in an oven full of farts, with a shit-fueled fire, then they served it with a tall glass of ass and vomit."

There's a thump on the other side of the door into Hedra's office. Flora steps back instinctively. "Ègwen?"

The door bursts into pieces. Plastic shards fly in every direction, and a brown-shrouded figure leaps out of the room. As the shrapnel settles, the figure stops and looks down at Flora, who's on her back, eyes wide and locked on them. Their face is covered in brown cloth, except for a set of brown goggles. They have a masculine build under their shroud.

Ègwen emerges from the door, and the

shrouded figure runs down the hall.

Èdgwen moves as if to chase the shrouded figure for a moment, but stops over Flora. "Are you okay?" Èdgwen asks. She reaches down to give Flora a hand up.

"I'm fine," Flora says, waving her away. "Go get that bastard. For Bort."

"For Bort," Èdgwen says, and she leaves her friend on the ground as she chases after the person in the brown shroud.

Benkle claws and climbs through the dark tunnel, through roots and slime molds, toward the light and what sounds like a waterfall. The exit to the hole is in a mound of dirt at the base of an evergreen. Benkle's head pops out of the hole, and he gasps for air in an embarrassing manner.

Benkle sees Ferele and Huck on the shore. Poyo flies in small circles in his pink-bellied, purple-dragon form. Benkle waves his arms to get their attention, but they don't see him. He hollers, "Ferele! Huck!" but they don't hear him. Poyo lands and looks over at him, but Huck talks at Ferele over the sound of Benkle's yells. The twenty-foot tall waterfall not far behind them doesn't help.

They are across a large, flat boulder. To one side it drops into the water, and on the other the forest is thick, and the woods rustle with the movements of predation.

"Great," Benkle says. "Another rock."

A weasel drags a tiny alien carcass out of the woods, covered in its yellow hemolymph, and a saber-toothed rabbit pounces on the weasel, snapping its neck with a drop kick before it slices into it with its saber teeth. Benkle looks toward the glacier. It's still barely visible between the leaves of the upper canopy. If he could reach that, he could find the teleportal easily, and he'd probably find a lot fewer animals that want to eat him.

A worm with oversized eyes slithers out of the hole Benkle came from. While Benkle watches, paralyzed with fear, the worm does its little happy dance before it approaches him with a dreadful purpose.

Distressing bubbles rise from the lake a few feet from the shore above a large, dark patch of water, and the forest rustles with concealed entities. The cavernous angler's worm closes in. Benkle pants while his stomach growls. Without any food or body fat, Benkle's body has been eating his own muscles for fuel.

If he tries to cross the boulder, and it turns out to be just another rock-like monster, this one might kill him. The forest has proven itself to be full of dangers, almost taking his life at least three times today. One more would probably do the trick. He points his fully open eyes at the darkness in the water, maybe some massive, wide-set, rock-like alligator, or some freshwater breed of giant cephalopod. There are no good options between the land and the water, and Benkle would question the air if he could fly. The worm reaches all the way out of the hole in the ground, toward Benkle.

Benkle trepidatiously steps away from the worm and onto the rock. If he's light footed, maybe he can cross whatever creature this boulder almost certainly is without waking it up, if it's asleep and not just waiting for him to do just that. Halfway across the rock, the worm stops, and starts slithering back into the hole.

At the far end of the boulder, Benkle looks back at the worm's retreat, and down at the rock, realizing that it is just a rock. Benkle breathes a deep sigh of relief and turns back around just in time to see Poyo just before it tackles him.

"Oh, hey, Benkle!" Ferele says. She waves enthusiastically, grinning ear to ear. She cocks her head and points at his foot. "Where is your shoe?"

Benkle looks at his big toe, sticking out of his black sock. "I'll tell you later. While I'm good and drunk." He bends down, pulls his other shoe from his foot, and tosses it to the side. Poyo dives on the shoe, performs a downward dog with the shoe in its mouth, and lies down before it proceeds to chew on Benkle's shoe.

"As I was saying," Huck raises his voice, "there are some very important things you need to know." Huck steps close to Ferele and lowers his voice. "First and foremost, I've regretted not asking you this long before you went missing—"

"I'm missing?" Ferele asks.

"Yeah." Benkle says, nodding.

"Oh." Ferele says. "I guess I haven't slept."

Benkle says, "You were due back with the Scapi client two months ago."

"Oh shit," Ferele says, as if it's only mildly unusual. "Well, I guess that makes a little sense." She looks back up at Huck and asks, "What did you want to ask, Huck?"

"Will you have dinner with me?"

"Ha!" Ferele raises her fist to her lips to stifle any further laughter. Huck's wounded expression brings indescribable joy to Benkle, as he full-on belly laughs. It's contagious, and in a moment, both of them are laughing at Huck uncontrollably. Huck's cheeks flush, his head drops, and he turns away in shame. All of that only amplifies Benkle's laughter, and then Ferele's.

"Seriously though," Benkle says, cutting off their laughter, "there is some horrible shit going down." He eyes the treeline and scans the sky. "Can we talk about it on the way off this fucking planet?"

Ègwen chases the brown-shrouded person through the building. She says, "I know it's you, you asshole! Bort was our friend! You could not have found a nicer guy, and you . . . This was going on long before the wizard sickness! You don't get to use that excuse. And do you have any idea what your duplicate put me through, you psycho?" Ègwen turns a corner to find the person she's chasing has stopped.

The shrouded figure kneels over the floor, drawing on it with a thick marker, and in two seconds flat, they're done. They slap the spell with an open palm, and the black mark on the floor disappears, and something else appears from nothing. A tiny, flaming figure forms from thin air. It's a miniscule infernal beast, a fire-elemental chihuahua.

Ègwen stops in her tracks. That was fast.

The shrouded person draws a second spell with their other hand, which Ègwen now realizes has its own marker. The caster is done in two seconds. He drops the marker and puts his hand on the circle. Another fiery anklebiter appears.

Ègwen watches in shock and horror, and a wee bit of amusement, as the shrouded person picks up the marker and draws another spell circle, and another. Two at once. In a matter of moments, the caster has half a dozen tiny terrors in a semi-circle around him. One takes a step forward and barks.

Ègwen takes a slow, careful step back. She backs around the corner until it would obstruct her vision to go any farther. She stands with her hand on the wall, peeking around the edge while the shrouded caster stands and runs the other way down the hall. The hot chihuahuas follow, leaving tiny flaming pawprints.

Benkle picks the map up off the ground and glances up at a gray beast flying overhead. Quietly, he says, "We should try to get my gun on the way back." He turns his head and says, "Poyo, you have our backs, right?" but Poyo is well behind the group, sniffing a giant, purple-and-white passionflower.

"Where is your gun?" Ferele asks, oblivious to her volume and the danger everywhere around them.

"By the"—Benkle looks down at the map—"Maybe River estuary, in the woods."

Ferele asks, "Why did you leave your gun in the woods?"

Benkle says, "I was trying to save you from a

giant snake."

"What?" Ferele asks skeptically.

Huck says, "He was trying to save himself from a fishcrab."

Benkle puts his left hand on his hip and holds the map against the other. "I can do both."

"You didn't do either," Huck says.

Ferele asks, "What are you talking about, 'giant snake'?"

"We saw you in the woods," Benkle says. "Your foot was stuck. A snake came up behind you and swallowed you whole. I assume you teleported out or something."

Ferele says, "I teleported out of a . . . whatever it's called. My foot got stuck. That's the last time I teleported anywhere. I don't remember any snake, though."

Benkle looks to Ferele in recollection. "That's when the snake snuck up on you! You must have cast it at just the right time. Huck, back me up."

Huck says, "No."

A cool breeze comes down the hill, making the canopy sway and the humans shiver, especially Huck, only adding to the foulness of his mood.

"What?" Benkle asks. "Why?"

Huck lowers his voice and says between the chattering of his teeth, "I hate you. This is for laughing at me." He speaks up so Ferele can hear, teeth still chattering. "I don't have a clue what he's talking about." Huck steps forward, leading them along the shore. Ferele follows, glancing back and forth between them as she passes Benkle. Poyo leaps off the ground and glides toward them on its outstretched wings.

Benkle turns a scowl on Huck's back and glances at the lake. The bubbling, dark figure in the water doesn't need to do anything but exist there to encourage Benkle to pick up his step. He passes Ferele and leans in toward Huck. He lowers his voice and says, "I hope something out here eats you." His stomach growls and he raises his voice. "Do either of you have any food?"

The group approaches the Maybe River, down the shore from the house Ferele trespassed in.

"Wizard sickness . . ." Ferele says, shaking her head. "What the fuck?"

Benkle says, "Poyo, I'm expecting you to protect us until I can get my gun. Alright?"

Poyo lands and gives Benkle a big grin.

Huck says, "Poyo can barely do anything in the Real."

Poyo suddenly transforms into a two-foot-wide frog and flips Huck the bird. It looks back at Benkle and becomes the happy purple-dragon thing again. Its grin reminds Benkle of nothing so much as a pitbull.

Poyo and the group of humans proceed along the riverside. The humans avoid any round, flat rocks, but Poyo steps right on a fishcrab and cracks its spine. A bunch of other rocks turn up to look at the cartoon beast, and Poyo leaps into the air, leaving the fishcrabs to turn on the humans.

Ferele steps up into the woods to avoid the fishcrabs, and Huck and Benkle follow.

"Crazy," Ferele says. "I wonder if that's why the local druids have been pissing off all the animals."

"The fishcrabs?" Benkle asks.

"Them too, of course," Ferele says.

Benkle squints at Ferele and asks, "What?"

Ferele says, "The Wizard Sickness."

Huck steps around a short conifer and asks, "Local druids have been pissing off all the animals?"

"At least," Ferele says, "I think that's what the person said. I haven't exactly mastered the dialect of L Town Twee. I don't even know what their language is called. Come to think of it, I guess the Wizard Sickness explains quite a few things, like Bishhop trying to kill me."

Benkle stops in his tracks. "He tried to kill you?"

"Yeah," Ferele says, stopping next to Benkle. She grits her teeth and pulls her conical denim hat off her head. "I kind of stranded him on Gravita."

"You what?" Huck asks, catching up behind them. They proceed up the hill, with the Maybe River to their left.

"I only left for five minutes," Ferele says. "I needed a break from his colognes. When I returned, he was gone."

"Did you look for him?" Huck asks.

"Yeah, yeah," Ferele says. "Not very hard, mind you, but despite my moderate efforts, I found him. Then we checked into the local office. That's when he tried to kill me, and I decided that client could go duck himself."

"Where did you leave him?" Benkle asks.

Ferele says, "Gravita."

"I knew it!" Huck says, raising his fist in his first pseudo-triumph in quite some time.

Ferele says, "The Feudal Monarchy of the Lowest Golden Valley. I think we—we'd just gotten to Greensville?"

"Greensville . . . Is there a teleportal in Greensville?" Huck asks.

"How the fuck should I know?" Benkle asks.

"Teleport-*al*?" Ferele asks.

Benkle says, "They are an old-fashioned, science-based method of interstellar travel."

"Oh," Ferele says. "I wonder if Bish-hop knows they exist. I did not. What are they again?"

"You'll see one soon," Huck says. "Come to think of it, I didn't know what they were until I got to the auction the other day."

"That was months ago," Benkle says. They approach a short cliff face. Benkle opens the map and glances at it momentarily before folding it back up and proceeding.

Ferele tilts her head. "So, from what you guys are saying, it sounds like Bish-hop has this Wizard Sickness as well."

Benkle nods and says, "He's probably crazy."

Ferele puts her hand against the rock face and says, "Don't be ableist."

Benkle grimaces. "I have the Wizard Sickness."

"Oh," Ferele says. "Sorry to hear that. Still, a lot of people are triggered by that term."

Benkle says, "Sorry. I know I shouldn't use that term, but it's hard to remember sometimes. It feels like it's been beaten into my skull. Still, sorry."

Ferele puts her hand to her chin and says, "I guess that explains why Bish-hop tried to set that chariot driver on fire."

Huck says, "It sounds like he is just an asshole."

Benkle says, "Assholery is a symptom."

"Really?" Huck asks.

Benkle asks, "Did you not read the pamphlet?"

"How many symptoms are there?" Ferele asks.\

Benkle opens his mouth to answer, but the flying beast returns. With skin like a rock, dragonfly wings, six lion-like legs, and an array of tusks and tentacles for a head, it is the single most terrifying thing Benkle's been subjected to on this planet.

His horror-stricken gaze alerts Ferele and Huck to look, and she immediately bends down and starts drawing a spell in a patch of dirt, but Benkle stops her with a hand on her shoulder. He says, "Poyo, do you think you can take it?"

Poyo is busy sniffing another passionflower. Benkle's heart feels like it's stopped beating, awaiting his imminent death. Despite what feels like nonexistent blood flow, with no food in his stomach, Benkle chooses flight over freeze. He turns and runs away from the beast. Huck and Ferele freeze, and the beast passes them, chasing Benkle.

"Poyo!" Benkle shouts, approaching the purple-dragon creature as fast as he can. Poyo gets one look at the beast and turns into its intimidating, frightened form, entirely composed of sharp, black spikes dripping with poison, all of which would be super helpful, if Poyo could move at all in this form. Benkle mourns his last chance at survival as he runs past the useless elecre, and the monster stops to sniff Poyo before he follows Benkle deeper into the woods.

Benkle weaves through trees, leaps around boulders. He picks up rocks when his hands have to touch the ground, and he throws them at his assailant, as well as the occasional fishcrab. It only proceeds slowly, and Benkle has the supremely unsettling feeling that the beast might be toying with him. Not only is he about to die, but the monster probably isn't going to make it quick.

When he comes to a cliff face, he runs alongside it to pull more rocks to throw at the beast that looks like a rock. He pulls a rock down twice as big as his own head and smashes it on that of the beast, who catches it in its tentacles and breaks it into pieces in its grip. Benkle sees the beast's eyes for the first time, bulbous, glossy, black orbs that reflect Benkle's image, even as they convey a very alien rage.

The rest of the group is nowhere to be seen. The monster swipes at him with its forepaw and tosses him against a conifer. It rears up to pounce, and Benkle slips around the tree just in time for it to shield him against the beast's claws, which rip through the bark, inches into the trunk.

Benkle turns and runs as fast as his shoeless feet can carry him, unaware of and apathetic about where he is running. When he realizes this, Benkle clings to the tree branches to stop his forward momentum as his legs take him over the edge of the short cliff. His feet kick and search for footing until his body sways back to the cliff, and he can put his feet down beneath himself. He looks back to see the rock monster approaching faster than Benkle could ever hope to run.

Benkle jumps off the short cliff and lands a

few feet from his gun. He collapses and heaves for the breath that was knocked out of him. The monster looks down at him from the top of the cliff. It leaps off the cliff, spreading its wings to glide down. Benkle reaches for the gun and points it at the beast.

The rock monster opens its mouth to reveal pink flesh and rows of needle teeth. It swallows Benkle's gun, hand, and forearm, and its venomous fangs sink into the flesh above Benkle's elbow.

Benkle fires, and the beast drops dead. He pulls his gun out of the mouth of the beast, and his hand comes back covered in sticky mucus. His arm is already numb from the venom, so Benkle takes the weapon in his off hand.

When Huck and Ferele look down from the top of the cliff in apprehension, Benkle raises his weapon toward Huck and pulls the trigger. Nothing happens. "Damn it!" Benkle says. He whips most of the mucus off the gun with a wild arm motion, spraying the nearby rocks and fishcrabs, and he tries to fire at Huck again and again and again. "DAMN IT!!!"

With only the coronas of the red giant lighting the permafrost, which is sparsely covered in conifers, they approach the teleportal. They step up toward the frozen, pentagon-shaped teleportal, and the spruce guarding it, who frowns down at them. Benkle walks up to the tree-person and pays the fee for traveling.

"Holy shit!" Ferele says. "That fee is outrageous! I'd almost rather use a spell."

Benkle desperately wants to say something like *Don't you think that's a little crazy?* He bites his lip instead.

As they step up to the gate, Huck says, "If you think that's something, you should see the price of mythral."

"Oh," Ferele asks, "that stuff that doesn't teleport?"

Benkle types the code into the pale-blue console of the teleportal.

"Yeah," Huck says, "among other things. Benkle and I got some from Brance Heldinger. She was one of our clients. We got to show her a bunch of places in New Old Excellon City, and"—Huck takes Ferele's elbow excitedly—"we even got to drink with her!"

Ferele's freckled smile lights up, and she asks, "What was that like?"

Benkle stops typing, and a white glow appears in the center of the pentagon.

Huck opens his mouth but Benkle takes this perfect opportunity to direct his compulsion to insult away from Ferele. "Huck cried when we had to trade the apartment he was squatting in for some mythral."

"Hey!" Huck says, stopping just before the blue glow. "I had a butt bug and you know it!"

Benkle, Ferele, and the ent all laugh, each with a hand or limb covering their mouth.

Huck scowls and says, "Uhhh!" Then he looks toward the sun and asks, "Were we supposed to do something else while we were here?"

Benkle says, "Shut up," and he steps through the teleportal.

When they step out of the teleportal into the Solscapes tower, the sky is red, and the city bustles with hovertraffic. They come out of the glitching blue digital display, all ducking to prevent a horizontal reintry.

Mrs. Lotterydale is waiting for them in a milk-chocolate-and-pink-ombre outfit, from her contacts to her accessories. Her wig is in the form of cat-ear buns, pink in the very front, brown on the sides and back. She's standing behind the bar. Mrs. Lotterydale pours herself a drink of clear liquid with lime-green beads and asks, "Did you get the job done?"

As the teleportal starts to shut down, the digital wave display goes in and out, and the machine clinks and thunks, and its gears grind against each other. Benkle suddenly remembers what they were sent to Diadox to do. He and Huck gulp simultaneously, as the blood and fear rise on their faces.

Ferele looks at Huck and Benkle, taking in their terrified, red-faced expressions at a glance, and then she turns toward Mrs. Lotterydale, whose face is scary. Something causes Ferele to slowly collapse with an expression that says she'd rather be anywhere but right there, and she might as well go to sleep. And she does, stretched out on the floor in front of the teleportal, with her little conical hat on the floor next to her. Maybe it was Mrs. Lotterydale's scowl, or the hate in her eyes, or maybe the temperature shift after leaving the base of the glacier; it probably has something to do with the wizard sickness, or it could be a side effect of the solar flare interfering with the old, broken machine that just built them, but all of them feel . . . weird.

Mrs. Lotterydale sighs and takes a drink: half the glass in one gulp.

Huck says, "We were assaulted by fishcrabs and giant snakes," shrinking away from Mrs. Lotterydale toward the clunking, clamoring machine behind him.

Mrs. Lotterydale looks to Benkle and asks, "Is this so?" She waits, and Benkle opens his mouth to speak, but no words come out. Mrs. Lotterydale finishes off her drink.

Finally, Benkle says, "I lost my weapon and my shoe and I got scared." He looks past Mrs. Lotterydale and the wall. "There were so many angry animals."

Huck interjects, "So many kinds of crabs."

"Rock mimics," Benkle says.

Huck says, "Snakes."

"And a penis monster," Benkle says.

"That's what I said," Huck says.

"A different kind of penis monster," Benkle says. "With a bunch of weird phallic antennae." Benkle puts his hands up to his head and wiggles a few fingers, and then he curls his forefingers in front of his mouth like a mandible: "Pincers"—he points at his upper lip—"and a penistache."

Huck looks at him and slowly shakes his head.

"You weren't there," Benkle says. "It was a diving beetle larva, just look it up, you'll see what I mean."

"Ha!" Mrs. Lotterydale says. "Try not to lose your weapon next time."

"Actually," Benkle says, "it broke when some —"

"Enough excuses." Mrs. Lotterydale takes a sip of her drink. She points at the teleportal with her middle finger while the rest cradle her glass. "I need you two to go back through that hole."

Mrs. Lotterydale looks down at Ferele, shakes her head, and says, "This Wizard Sickness." She sighs. "What a fucking pain."

"Can I go buy a new gun first?" Benkle asks.

Mrs. L. shakes her head. "No."

"I *need* shoes."

"Here." Mrs. Lotterydale takes off her brown-and-pink-ombre flats. "They may look better on you, but I want them back."

"Where are we going?" Benkle asks.

Mrs. Lotterydale says, "Gravita."

"Bish-hop of Ihs is on Gravita," Huck says.

"That is correct, surprisingly, and you two need to rescue him and get me the reward for his return."

"What?" Benkle asks with a snarl. "Did you break and drink the last of your possessions again, you rotting bag of ambergris and dog—" Benkle's eyes pop open as he locks them with Mrs. Lotterydale's, who's blinking and still processing what all Benkle just said. "Shit!"

Ègwen sits in a folding chair beside the shattered door into Hedra's office, where the body and—she assumes—the brain of Bort still lie. She's made her own caution tape out of duct tape she got from an engineer and half the staff supply of black markers.

Cotl comes down the hall saying, "You are relieved, Miss Bideon. Mrs. Lotterydale wants to ask you about all this." Cotl gestures toward the empty doorframe. "She's in the teleportal room."

"Really?" Ègwen asks. "They sent you?"

"I tried to tell them they were wasting their money." Cotl stops to take in the shattered door pieces and the half attempt at mopping the line of vomit leading from the door to the brain on the office floor. "Looks like things have remained eventful."

Ègwen nods and stands, stretching her limbs.

"So you saw him?" Cotl asks.

Ègwen puts her arms down and says, "I saw someone. I don't know if it was a man."

"But you suspect . . . ?"

"Oh," Ègwen says, "it almost certainly was one man in particular."

"Hedra."

"Hedra." Ègwen nods. "Same build. Same height. In his office. It's all a little obvious." Ègwen stops herself, and her eyes dart around in thought. "I don't mean to be a gossip—it still might not be Hedra. We really shouldn't make that assumption . . ." Ègwen's open-mouthed expression suggests that she's not so sure about what she just said. She reaches into her pocket. "But there is someone who needs to hear about this. She pulls out her phone. A notification between two exclamation points is at the center of her screen: "!Service Restored!"

Ègwen clicks the hang-up button and talks to herself in a mocking tone: "'We'll get there when we get there.' Fucking cops."

Ègwen pushes open the door to the com room. The room itself seems to hum, all but inaudibly, and the noise grows imperceptibly louder. Ègwen sniffs. It smells more like plastic than the last time she was here. Glancing around the room, then to her right, at an empty chair, Ègwen can see that the attendant is not there, as usual. Ègwen sighs and starts examining pedestal labels, searching for the right one.

The room is as big as a gymnasium, full of randomly dispersed pedestals, each of them holding a crystal, either translucent blue or citrine yellow. The hum rises ever so slowly.

Just as Ègwen gets close enough to read the labels below the nearest crystals, they all start to vibrate. She watches on, slack jawed, as all the crystals in the room tremble in unison on their pedestals until, as one, they explode. Crystal pieces fly a few feet in every direction from every pedestal, and a cloud of tiny fragments forms throughout the room.

Ègwen throws her arms up between the crystal shards and her eyes, and turns to run. She catches only a glimpse of the shrouded figure escaping through the com room doors. When she exits the room behind them, the figure is nowhere to be seen, and Ègwen stomps on the floor while shouting, "Ducking—Fucking—Fuck you, Hedra! You butt-faced . . . butthole! FUCK!!!"

With that out of her system, she says to herself, "Wow, Ègwen, you're really diving right into this whole swearing thing."

CHAPTER 7: AN UNNECESSARY EXPENDITURE

Mrs. L. asks, "What did you just say to me, Benkle?"

The room falls still. Benkle swallows. The guards by the door look at the walls, afraid of catching Mrs. Lotterydale's eyes and even a fraction of her wrath. Ferele is passed out in front of the teleportal, next to her conical hat. Huck tries to hide his grin. Meanwhile, Poyo moseys over to the window, lifts itself up by the frame, and looks out the window.

Benkle falls to his knees. He grovels, crawling toward Mrs. L. "It's the wizard sickness! It's how it's manifesting in me!" He clasps his hands together, pleading with his eyes for mercy.

"Cantankerous assholery, eh?" Mrs. Lotterydale eyes Benkle through milk-chocolate-and-pink-colored contacts. "You lucky fuck. I guess it's convenient that you assist Huck, then." She raises her hand in a dismissive gesture while she raises her glass in the other.

"So," Mrs. Lotterydale asks, "what have you two been doing on Diadox?"

"We found Ferele," Huck says, gesturing to where she's passed out on the floor next to her conical hat.

Benkle looks past Mrs. Lotterydale with a distant expression. "And a bunch of very hostile wildlife."

Mrs. Lotterydale moves a pink hair out of her face and says, "That's why you keep track of your gun, Benkle. You could have done all that *and* gotten the mythral like you were supposed to." She steps around the bar and walks toward the interstellar travelers.

Benkle stands frozen. He swallows and says, "We should have. Yes."

Mrs. Lotterydale grimaces at Benkle, stepping right up into his personal space. "You looked kind of like you wanted to insult me again for a moment." Benkle leans away from her as she invades his personal space. "As it is, your shit is not my problem. You better not make it my problem."

"I will never, ever do that again," Benkle says.

"That would be for the best," Mrs. Lotterydale says conversationally, "if you want to keep your hide and your job. Now, answer me another question. Where the fuck is the mythral box?"

Huck and Benkle look at each other in confusion, then terror.

Benkle turns to Huck and asks, "Is it still in the L Town Twee lake?"

Huck says, "That's the last I saw it."

"WHY THE FUCK IS IT IN THE LAKE!?" Mrs. Lotterydale asks. "No. Never mind." She walks back to the bar. "Just keep your mouths shut."

Mrs. Lotterydale picks up a bottle, mumbling to herself. "I could just disintegrate everything and everyone. That would solve all my problems."

Benkle swallows.

Huck does the unthinkable, and opens his fucking mouth. "I tried to c—"

Mrs. Lotterydale's eyes glow red with magic, and their shape distorts in hatred. "I could kill you with one look." Benkle's curious when and how Mrs. Lotterydale activated that prepared spell, and why she prepared the spell in the first place. What he should probably be wondering is how to get the hell out of this situation.

As it happens, a distraction comes through the doors in that instant in the form of a gorgeous woman with big hair, even in a ponytail. Employee Resources Director Égwen Bideon rushes in and doubles over. Between gasps for breath, she says, "The com crystals . . ." Everyone turns to face the newcomer. "They're all gone!"

"*What?!*" Mrs. Lotterydale demands.

"Shattered," Égwen says. She inhales deeply and stands up straight.

Mrs. Lotterydale goes into shock for a moment. Then a curious expression comes over her face, and she cocks her head, saying, "I thought you were supposed to come directly from Hedra's office to see me."

Égwen grits her teeth.

Mrs. Lotterydale's eyes narrow on Égwen like a predator who found its nest empty and the culprit inside. The Employee Resources Director shrinks back. Mrs. Lotterydale asks, "How am I supposed to know that you're not responsible for that *and* the murder?"

"I…" Égwen stammers. "You have access to the security feed."

"Actually," Mrs. Lotterydale says, "I shut that off to save money."

"Wait—" Huck says.

"There was a murder?" Benkle asks.

"Bort," Égwen and Mrs. Lotterydale say simultaneously.

"Oh no!" Benkle cries out.

"Why Bort?" Huck asks. "Who the fuck would . . . Oh."

Benkle's distant expression returns, and he says, "He is the only person working here that I can stand to be around for more than a few minutes at a time." Everyone in the room scowls at him. "Three-fourths . . ." He looks down at Ferele. "Four-fifths of present company excluded, of course."

It would seem Égwen's confidence is rising as she dares to raise her voice. "How dare you accuse me, after I nearly died chasing that asshole?"

"Whoa!" Mrs. Lotterydale throws her hand up, putting the brakes on this conversation, in desperate need of clarification, and at the same time as Huck and Benkle, she says, "You swear now?"

Égwen puts her hands on her hips. "Ever since I almost died at the hands of a duplicate of that asshole."

Mrs. Lotterydale steps right up to Égwen and says, "How dare *you* take that tone with *me?!*"

Benkle says, "I think all our tensions are running a little high right now. Maybe we should all step back and cool off."

Mrs. L. and Égwen both turn on the executive assistant. "Shut up, Benkle!"

Huck snickers. Benkle turns his glower on him. Huck says, "It's nice to see that happen to someone else for a change."

"Listen to me," Mrs. L. says. "All of you, if you value your jobs and your hides."

"Oh my!" Égwen exclaims as she covers her mouth in surprise. "Is that Ferele?!" She runs over to the teleportal to kneel over the denim-clad figure, who is sleeping next to her conical hat on the floor, snoring softly. "Shouldn't we do something?"

"She's okay," Mrs. Lotterydale says. "She didn't just have her life ripped out from under her." Mrs. L. shakes her head and narrows in on Benkle. "You need to get your shit together, or you are going to single-handedly let Huck ruin this company."

Benkle swallows. "Yes, ma'am."

Mrs. L. says, "Now, I need you two to go back through that hole there and find one of our missing clients."

Huck asks, "Any of our missing clients, or one in particular?"

Mrs. Lotterydale only responds to her son with a glare, and continues speaking as if he said nothing. "The last time they checked in was on Gravita, so you'll start there."

"Umm . . ." Benkle asks, "How are we supposed to withstand the gravity on a high-g world without the aid of magic?"

Mrs. Lotterydale says, "The teleportals are designed to make you able to withstand the conditions they bring you into."

Benkle says, skeptically, "I heard that only some of them work that way."

Mrs. Lotterydale shrugs and pulls a baggie of white powder out from her cleavage. "In that case . . ." She steps up to the group and holds the baggie out to the executive assistant. "Pure Excellonian megacoke."

Benkle grimaces and takes the baggie from Mrs. Lotterydale.

Huck says, "That's your cure-all for everything."

Mrs. Lotterydale snarls at her son and says, "I can't help it if it's a versatile drug. I'll take it back if you don't want it." She snatches the bag from Benkle's hand.

Huck snatches the baggy back from his mother and says, "I *never* said I didn't want it."

Mrs. Lotterydale turns toward the window and the purple dragon-like creature looking out of it, and she asks, "Poyo, how would you like to stay with me? It has been too long since I've gotten to see my favorite grandchild."

Poyo lumbers up to Mrs. Lotterydale and licks her hand. She reaches into her pocket and pulls out some treebacon. Poyo gobbles it up and lets its butt plop down next to her before opening its mouth in a wide, happy, hell-mouthed grin.

Ferele rolls over, mumbling something incoherent in her sleep. Égwen leans in close to hear, to no avail.

Benkle sits down on the hard floor next to Ferele and Égwen. Benkle rubs his tender foot arch and asks, "And what about the mythral on Diadox?"

Mrs. Lotterydale says, "I'll send the new guy. He seems capable enough, at least twice as capable as the two of you combined. He'll meet with David."

"Who's David?" Huck asks.

Mrs. L. puts her fingers into the space between her eyes. "Your contact in L Town. You idiot."

"You idiot." Benkle communicates all his hate with his eyes, but Huck doesn't look at him, deciding instead to shrug and rub his sole on a floor stain.

Mrs. L. turns her attention back to the seated Benkle. "You need to get your shit together."

Huck says, "You already said that."

Mrs. L. and Benkle turn on Huck: "Shut up, Huck!"

Mrs. Lotterydale shakes her head at her son. "Coming in late," she says, talking to Benkle, but looking her disappointment in the eyes. "You know Huck can't handle that much responsibility."

"Yes, ma'am," Benkle says.

Mrs. Lotterydale starts pacing. "The money to get the mythral box out of the lake is coming out of your paychecks, and if we can't find it, or it's broken, you two are buying us a new one."

Benkle stands up. "I can barely afford my wizard sickness treatments as it is."

"Oh." Mrs. Lotterydale pauses her pacing to ask over her shoulder. "What are you doing?"

"Blood infusions from the impotent," Benkle says.

"Is it helping?" Mrs. L. asks.

"I thought so for a while," Benkle says, "but now I think it was just a placebo."

"Yeah, same thing with reiki," Mrs. L. says. "Still, you're buying us a new mythral box."

"I still owe 50 octillion credits to Dr. Mitt Ritter. He said that if I'm late on my next payment, he'll take my liver and use it as part of a composite monster. He said something about me being

Faeish . . . Regardless, the man is going to take my liver!"

Mrs. Lotterydale stops pacing in front of Benkle to ask, "Well, whose problem is that?"

The room gets very quiet, very still. A bright light from outside the window passes over the tele-portal, and then Ferele and Égwen, Huck and Benkle, and lastly, Mrs. Lotterydale.

Benkle's head slumps, and he says, "It's mine."

Mrs. Lotterydale's eyebrow arches at Benkle. "Okay." She puts her left hand on her right elbow and gestures at the pair with her right hand. "Now, go to Gravita and find Bish-hop of Ihs. And Benkle"—Mrs. Lotterydale gestures down at the pink-and-chocolate-colored flats he's wearing—"I want my shoes back in perfect condition when you're done."

"Of course, ma'am," Benkle says.

"And Benkle." Mrs. Lotterydale crosses her arms. "If I ever hear you say anything like that comment to me again, you will pay dearly."

"I swear to you, Mrs. Lotterydale." Benkle's voice is sincere. His eyes are wide and genuine. "I will never—"

"Good," Mrs. Lotterydale interjects.

"—call you a narcissistic sack of shit anywhere where you can overhear."

Benkle nurses a fresh black eye as the teleportal in Greensville, on the planet Gravita, constructs him from local materials amidst a pink-colored digital liquid display. His hair falls straight down on his scalp, eliminating what wave there was to his black hair. His big toe sticks through one of his socks, on otherwise bare feet. He and Huck are instantly oppressed by the gravity in the Feudal Monarchy of the Lowest Golden Valley, but they are fueled by Excellonian megacoke, so they slowly collapse onto the cobblestone ground instead of suddenly.

"I'm so heavy!" Huck says, as he lies down on golden elemental grass in front of the square teleportal and a smirking Amazon guard in a white leather turtleneck. "Too heavy!"

Benkle groans and says, "This teleportal obviously doesn't prepare people for the high gravity." He pulls the bag of cocaine out of his pocket, and a straw, which he slides into the bag. He puts it up to his nose and inhales deeply. Benkle hands the bag to Huck, who reaches for it greedily.

Huck snorts.

Benkle says, "Whoa there. Don't shit yourself while you're away from your spare pants."

Huck laughs. "Ha!" He coughs and spits up

some of the coke. "Aagh! I feel like you could have waited for a better opportunity to drop that one, but I'm definitely going to have to steal it. Also, I don't have any other pants. I gave my spare pants away."

Benkle says, "That explains the smell." He picks himself up. The gold elemental grass is sharp on the bottoms of Benkle's unshod feet as he slouches toward the Amazonian teleportal guard, a dark-haired, dark-skinned beauty with a scar over her right eye and white leather armor covering her from neck to toe. She stands nine feet tall, with muscles defined even through her leather, and she points with her silver-etched spear at a sign depicting one hand putting five platinum-colored coins in another hand.

Benkle reaches into his pocket and presents the woman twice his height with a handful of platinum.

Huck groans as he picks himself up, then takes another snort through the straw. "Whoa!" He blinks a few times and zips up the baggie. He asks Benkle, "What do you think happens when you die?"

Benkle turns a curious look on his boss and starts walking along the cobblestone road, which leads between two tall, jagged mountains made almost entirely out of gold. Huck steps in line. Benkle says, "I met a ghost once. I asked him what happens in the afterlife."

Huck struggles against the pull of gravity to walk up to Benkle, asking, "What did he say?"

Benkle says, "'Don't die.'"

Huck chuckles and says, "According to the Primists, our souls go to either the star system Maledis or the Heavenly star system, depending on how good they were in life. Then they are further split into specific worlds, like Hell or the Abyss, depending on factors that vary depending on the religion. Elysium is super nice, but it's FULL of old people and narcissistic fuckboys that do nothing but party and scam the old people. And the angels . . . I hear that a lot of them are assholes."

Benkle rolls his eyes. "I was there when Heldinger gave us her life story."

Huck continues on as if Benkle never spoke. "Now, the Followers of Fate and the Protector worshippers both believe the afterlife is a hodgepodge reality, in part mirroring the living worlds, while the bulk of it is built by the dead themselves, mostly at the behest of dead deities. The Hurrasi"--Benkle sighs--"of Dragonthrone believe their spirit goes through something called a Glass Forest, into an arch-shaped portal that leads to three different afterlifes."

Benkle asks, "Why are you lecturing me about afterlife myths?"

Huck says, "I guess I'm just scared. The wizard sickness has me thinking, and this coke doesn't exactly stop the flow of thoughts. I'm never going to cast another spell again. Not even to save my own life."

Benkle says, "That is probably for the best. The last thing the world needs is people who are both stupid *and* insane."

Huck scowls at Benkle.

They step onto a cobblestone road leading between two jagged mountains. A tall man with khaki-colored skin approaches in the shadow of a mountain. He wears metal elemental furs, rubies, and gold, and it looks like it's been a few months since he's shaved or bathed.

"How are we going to recognize Bish-hop if we find him?" Huck asks.

Benkle pulls out his phone and unlocks it. The background is an image of his lover, Alfounz, and the buttons of his main screen are laid out on his naked abs and chest. He opens a folder marked "Work Files" while Huck ponders a large gold elemental king snake with the eyes of a deer in headlights. The snake slithers away, through the golden grass.

Benkle says, "Here," and shows Huck an image of Bish-hop of Ihs. His fists are on his hips, his head held high. He has beige skin and blue eyes. He wears a simple loop crown over graying black hair, a long yellow cape, and more rubies and gold than anyone else would ever think necessary.

As the mud-covered man on the road approaches twenty feet from Huck and Benkle, his smell reaches for them. At fifteen feet, the smell of foot and cologne becomes obnoxious. At ten, it overpowers. At five feet the pair hold their breath.

They all walk past each other, trying to avoid looking. After passing, Huck gasps for breath and asks Benkle, "How far to the local Solscapes office?"

The dirty man turns to face the pair and point at them, with blue eyes as wide and menacing as they get. "*YOU!*"

An overpoweringly odored man in dirty rubies and filthy gold says, "I know who you are!" He points a grubby finger at Huck and says, "Heir to Solscapes Interstellar Realty! Your family is responsible for me being stranded here!"

"Who the heck are you?" Huck asks.

Benkle puts a hand up to his face and sighs. "That's Bish-hop of Ihs."

Bish-hop extends his left hand in front of him and twists his palm while he snaps with his right fingers. His eyes burn like fire on Huck, who looks away in discomfort. Bish-hop brings both his hands to his right hip and rotates them as if there is an orb between them. He's activating a prepared spell.

Huck holds his hands up and says, "Whoa! It's not my fault that one of my employees went insane."

Bish-hop holds his stance for a moment: legs spread in warrior pose, left hand extended forward, limp, right hand at his waist. His head cocks to the side, and he says, "I have had my own share of employees lose their minds. Such weak people, the poor."

Huck smiles through the cologne and foot smell to ask, "Would you accompany us through the Greenville teleportal, so we can collect the reward for your return?"

Bish-hop's eyes grow intense again, and he asks in an equally intense voice, "*You think you deserve a* reward*?!*" Bish-hop snaps his left fingers and rotates his right wrist, completing the spell activation with a tiny burst of blue-and-yellow flame hovering above his right palm.

The flame grows into a fireball in Bish-hop's hand. The fireball expands even more as he pushes it at Huck, and it flies from his hand. The fireball grows into a firestorm as it flies straight toward Mr. Lotterydale. The firestorm moves harmlessly through the golden elemental plant life, straight toward a more flesh-covered individual.

Benkle leaps and pushes Huck out of the way. The Amazon raises her weapon and turns to face the group. Bish-hop's eyes and his wicked smile reflect the fireball

Benkle lands on top of Huck. Disgust erupts inside him. He wants to vomit, but instead he says, "Why the fuck did I just do *that*?" He crawls off of Huck and picks himself up.

Huck reaches for Benkle to give him a hand up, and Benkle slaps his hand away. Bish-hop starts activating another prepared fireball spell. He extends his left hand in front of him and twists his palm while he snaps with his right fingers. Huck looks up at Bish-hop in terror, and Benkle turns to confront the dirty warrior-CEO. Bish-hop brings both his hands to his right hip and rotates them as if there is an orb between them.

Benkle's tone lowers, and in a voice that gives pause to the most pompous person in three systems Benkle says, "*You can kill him when I'M done with him.*" and he turns back to Huck.

Huck says, "I'd rather not die at all."

Benkle shouts, "*You* don't get a choice in the matter!" and he kicks his boss in the ribs.

"Ow!" Huck shouts. He grabs his injured side.

Benkle considers for just a moment. *This is probably it. Mrs. Lotterydale would love the situation, but Huck would make my life miserable from now on.* He's past the point of no return. He kicks Huck in the ribs again. It hurts Benkle less than simply walking barefoot on gold elemental grass.

"You are the *worst!*" Benkle yells at his boss as he kicks him again and repeatedly. "Your sense of humor is *so* bad! I'd rather starve to death, alone and homeless, than spend another minute with you! That noise you make when you fall asleep at the desk makes me want to claw out my eardrums and stab you in your ugly face! If I ever see you again, I will stab you in your ugly face!"

The Amazon glances down at them in half interest, leaning on her spear.

Benkle lands one more kick to Huck's ribs. Huck whimpers softly. Benkle turns to Bish-hop and asks, "I see that you are alone. You wouldn't happen to be in need of a new assistant?"

Bish-hop produces a wide grin and steps up to Benkle to put a thick-fingered hand on Benkle's shoulder. Benkle struggles to keep his nose from wrinkling at the smell, and opens his mouth slightly to breathe through it. "I am," Bish-hop says, "and I find you quite amusing, but I would never let anyone talk to me the way you just spoke to your employer."

Huck holds his side and winces, saying, "Benkle's like this all the time, not the physical abuse, but the verbal. It's just nonstop."

Bish-hop grins ear to ear.

Benkle says to his former boss, "Your incompetence is excruciating."

Bish-hop says, "I really can't blame you for treating such a pathetic excuse for a person like such a pathetic excuse for a person. Send me your resume, and I'll put in a good word for you with some of my least-favorite peers."

"Thanks . . ." Benkle says. "I guess."

"Oh my gods!" Huck shouts, struggling to get up off the ground. He rolls over onto his stomach and fails to do a pushup. "I hate Gravita!"

Benkle shakes his head and crosses his arms. Bish-hop of Ihs laughs jovially. Even the Amazon looks down at the Monrician in the dirt and chuckles.

Huck reaches toward Benkle's feet and says, "Please, help me Benkle. Get me back to the tele-portal safely and I'll give you a 10 percent raise."

This time Benkle is the one laughing. "Nowhere near enough."

Huck crawls toward Benkle, begging. "Twenty percent!" He grunts as he lifts his torso off the ground. "And I'll never antagonize you again! I swear it! Twenty-five!"

Benkle reaches down and takes Huck's arm and his collar, and lifts him up by both until Huck is on his knees, looking up into Benkle's eyes.

"Huck you," Benkle says, and he pushes Huck back over onto the ground. "I quit."

CHAPTER 8: THE PLOT THINNENS

"HA!" Bish-hop of Ihs laughs, pointing at the fallen President of Solscapes Interstellar Realty. Huck remains on the ground, nursing his wounds while Benkle disappears into the pink digital display of the square teleportal.

Bish-hop says, "He used your name in place of fuck because you're such a fucking fuck-up! I'm *so* glad I got that on camera! You're going to be famous on *MeTube*. HA! You are *so* pathetic!"

Bish-hop stands over Huck and offers him his hand. Huck takes it, and Bish-hop puts his dirty boot and the source of the foot smell on Huck's neck. "You owe me," he says in a low, quiet voice.

A cloud passes between them and the sun, and the heavy air chills.

"You're going to find me a continent for sale. *Zero* commission. With a sizable human population. No less than ten million. Some place where people aren't so fucking crazy. People are *fucking crazy* here." Bish-hop briefly, timidly meets the eyes of the teleportal guard.

Huck says, "The margins on continents are already so thin, between mapping updates, population modeling, and with the wizard si—"

"Shut the *Huck* up!" Bish-hop says, leaning on Huck's neck and twisting his wrist. Huck's face turns purple. His struggle to breathe produces a croaking noise. It would be easy enough for Bish-hop to just lean in a little more. Gravity would do the rest.

"Ha!" Bish-hop throws Huck's wrist to the ground and removes his foot from Huck's neck. While Huck gasps for air, Bish-hop says, "I like that. 'Shut the Huck up.'" Bish-hop steps toward the teleportal. "You really might be famous one day."

Huck struggles against gravity to pick himself up, coughing, with dirt falling off him as he slowly rises.

"I still expect that continent," Bish-hop says.

Huck says, "We—" he coughs over his response.

Bish-hop takes a purse from underneath his cape and hands it to the Amazon.

Huck painfully steps up behind Bish-hop and asks, "You haven't come across any mythral, have you?"

"All I have left is this purse of mythral coins," Bish-hop says, plugging the code into the flat side of the teleportal, "and I'll be Hucked if you're coming anywhere near them . . ." The teleportal opens with a pink digital display.

". . . you stupid piece of sh—" Bish-hop is removed from this place by the teleportal, and the mythral contents fall out of his bag as it's teleported alongside him; the coins remain on Gravita and fall into the gold elemental grass.

A bolt of lightning strikes in the distance. The Amazon looks off into that distance, at a particularly tall, particularly jagged mountain, while Huck looks back and forth between her and the mythral coins on the ground: maybe a few more than a dozen. Maybe a little more than a pound of mythral.

Lightning strikes the peak of another mountain in the distance, distracting the toll guard, so Huck picks up the coins. He just now realizes that a pound is not a pound on Gravita as he struggles and fails to lift a handful of the coins. He softly grunts, and stops. Eyeing the Amazon, Huck picks the coins up one at a time. He slips them into his quickly sagging pockets. He tightens his belt.

The Amazon turns her head back toward Huck, but another strike draws her attention away, and Huck picks up the last of the coins, thick, round, hollow coins with intricate, monstrous hieroglyphs around the mostly empty middle. The mostly hollow center of each coin features an L-shaped stretch of mythral with bas reliefs depicting the faces of the last seven queens of the Feudal Monarchy of the Lowest Golden Valley.

The Amazonian shakes her head at Huck as he lumber-shuffles down the cobblestone path toward the local Solscapes office, seventeen miles east-northeast, through the oncoming storm. She glances west, where a pair of battling dragons in the far distance break the side of a mountain.

"I'm so proud of you," Benkle's phone tells him from the break-room counter in the raspy voice of his boyfriend, Alfounz. Benkle's face is buried in the fridge. Three other people are shoved into this tiny space. An ogre in a Staff t-shirt plays the card game Sorcerers with a gorgeous, rabbit-eared, semi-symmetrical devi. A two-inch-tall tree gnome hangs in a harness halfway up the side of a two-foot-wide counter, hammering a spike into the worldwood finish, climbing to the top and to the bean-juice maker it holds.

"Where the hell is my steak and sprout balls?" Benkle asks, as if Alfounz can help him from across town. "I swear, if that stiffsock ate my balls, I'm going to quit!"

"You just did," Alfounz says. "That's why I'm

so proud of you. Money isn't everything. Your well-being *is* everything."

Benkle grits his teeth. "Money is how you buy everything. The correlation between money and well-being is extremely high . . ." Benkle stands up, and his head and shoulders slump down. "Money really is everything . . . Fuck! What did I do?"

Alfounz takes a moment to switch gears and says, "You escaped a sinking ship." There's a click or maybe a clink on Alfounz's end of the call. "You had an incredible amount of loyalty just to stay this long. Any company would be ecstatic to have you on their team."

The ogre and the devi chuckle. Benkle meets the ogre's eyes for a moment with a glance that tells the ogre to mind his own fucking business, and he does. The ogre draws a card and avoids looking at Benkle.

Benkle pulls a clear plastic box marked "BENKLE CHERRYBLOSSOM" from beneath a soggy plastic bag full of rotting, gelatinized potatoes. A single pair of sprout balls is all that remains. The barbeque sauce has been licked off the edge, Huck's trademark move; he left a few of his beard hairs, his calling card. This must have been right before he shaved, or maybe right after. Benkle bares his teeth in rage and shakes his fist at the meal, wishing it was Huck's face, and that he was beating it to death.

Alfounz says, "You'll probably make more money right away than Solscapes would ever give you . . . with your magical capabilities."

Benkle stops waving his arms at the contents of his box of leftovers, and his eyes widen like an animal backed into a corner. "About that," Benkle says. "I need to tell you something."

Benkle tosses his leftovers back in the fridge while he ponders how to say what he needs to say, and Alfounz waits patiently on the other end of the line. Benkle closes the door carefully, like he's afraid of making any noise.

"What is it?" Alfounz asks, concern filling his voice.

"I don't know how to say it," Benkle says.

"Just say it," Alfounz says, unaware that Benkle is in a small room full of four people.

"Today was the worst day . . . Oh my gods, Alfy . . ." Benkle tears up. "I have to tell you something horrible . . ."

The inhale Alfounz draws as he braces for this impact is audible over the phone.

Benkle sighs and says, "Bort passed away."

The devi and the ogre and even the tree gnome, who is just reaching the top of the counter, each shed a tear for the dearly departed, and wipe them away.

"What?!"

"How the hell," Benkle asks Égwen, as they walk through the lavender hall, "did Mrs. L. get everyone to give up the new break room?" Benkle tries to avoid eye contact as they walk past Mrs. Lotterydale's office. Mrs. Lotterydale sits at a faux-crystal desk in her old office, which was once the board room and is now her office again. She puts her stylus down and glares at Benkle.

Égwen also averts her eyes and whispers one word to Benkle covertly: "Fear." She steps ahead and opens the door for Benkle, out to the garage. Huck's egg-shaped cherry-red hovercar is double-parked in his space.

"Fuck!" Benkle puts his hand on his face. "My hovercar is parked at the next entrance down."

"I'll give you a ride," Égwen says.

"Can you talk the garage out of charging me for every day I was teleportaling?" Benkle asks.

"I'm sorry," Égwen says. "Not since the bank took most of the building from the Lotterydales." Égwen holds her hovercar door open for Benkle.

Benkle gets inside, Égwen shuts the door behind him, and a warning flashes on the dashboard in front of the passenger seat. "Danger! Buckle your harness! Space travel is perilous!" Benkle pulls the harness down from above and straps four buckles and a lot of thick, heavy fabric across his chest. Égwen opens the driver's-side door, slips in, and shuts the door before she says, "It is *really* lucky that you got out now." She straps herself in and asks, "Can I share a secret with you?"

"Of course," Benkle says. "I told you about my Lip Heldinger dreams."

Égwen waves her hand dismissively. "Autopilot, take us to the next garage down." She turns to face Benkle. "Everyone has dreams like that about Lip Heldinger. Even straight men."

Benkle opens his mouth, but he has no response. He just blinks.

The hovercar gently lifts from its position and moves out of the parking space.

Égwen says, "There's a duplicate of me running around somewhere."

Benkle cocks his neck and asks Égwen, "Come again?"

"Truthfully, I'm the duplicate," Égwen says. "The original me quit Solscapes months ago. I was created by Hedra, alongside a duplicate of himself, to search for Ferele when she went missing. Good job finding her, by the way. I searched all over the Lowest Golden Valley, but I never found her *or* Bishhop."

The hovercar exits the electroshielding, entering the black void that is the "atmosphere" of Monric. The car drops at a slowish, steadying rate, about a floor per second. Benkle looks on at Égwen expectantly.

Égwen says, "Very, very long story short, I

got Hedra's duplicate to make me permanent, and I came back to Monric. The original me had quit, but I didn't know that yet." The hovercar passes the toll android, and the sticker on her windshield marked "Robopass" lights up in a soothing shade of blue. The hovercar veers away from the building, toward the end of the orderly line of hovering cars reaching into the middle tower garage, as random hovercars fly out of the garage in a chaotic fashion. "I went home to find out that my apartment had exploded."

"My first thought was for my family. They're safe, though. They thought I was dead. My second thought was that Hedra was probably responsible for all of this. His duplicate was incredibly hostile on Gravita, and he was talking to someone that wasn't there. Now that I know about the wizard sickness . . . it complicates things a little, but the more I think about it, the more I'm sure that he's guilty of Bort's murder."

Benkle shakes his head. "That fucking . . ." He clenches his fist.

Égwen continues: "A lot of people have been weird around me, though, ever since I got back from Gravita. The new guy, Ren, definitely has some profound issues with the wizard sickness, so part of me wondered if it was him. Flora's been distant. Mrs. Lotterydale is an obvious candidate. She's been especially ornery recently, although that could just be all the stress of her company falling to shit and her addiction to red magic. That fucking woman."

"Is that some sort of duplicate thing?" Benkle

asks. "The only way to tell you apart is that you swear."

They reach the end of the line of hovercars, behind a gremlin carpooling with a hobbit.

"Trust me," Égwen says, "if Original Égwen had lived through the things I've lived through, she'd be doing it too. Not every member of my family approves, though."

Benkle asks, "Do you think Original Égwen ended up in the explosion?"

Égwen shakes her head. "That's what I thought at first. There was no death certificate, though. She would have had to be right in the middle of the explosion . . ."

Benkle says, "That would mean that someone *was* trying to kill her."

Égwen says, "That's what she said when I found her."

"Oh," Benkle says. He blinks, processing the mystery unfolding.

"It was right after you left for Gravita. Hedra had just killed Bort and disappeared, and I ran into myself while I was at my favorite bean-juice cafe."

A large, hovering truck with a penguin at the wheel pulls up behind them in line. A honk from somewhere nearby comes over the short-wave radio as the line hovers in place.

Égwen says, "She said that we couldn't be seen together, and she split. I searched for weeks. I'm still searching for her, actually." The line proceeds slowly toward the middle entrance of the building. A falling spaceship collides with a hovercar halfway between them and the front of the line, the one behind them fills in the gap, and the line moves forward until it can't anymore. It hovers in place again.

Égwen says, "I've yet to curse anyone out so much as I did myself that day. It started a big fight with my husband. He doesn't know what's going on, just that I was missing, our house exploded, and that I swear now."

The line moves forward.

"So, then Flora comes to me yesterday, and she spilled everything. Mrs. Lotterydale paid Hedra to kill the other version of me."

"What the hell for?" Benkle asks.

"That," Égwen says, "I don't know . . . She said I was safe, but I'll tell you what . . ." She looks around at the clockwork motions of hovering traffic moving in and out of skypiercer towers, and down, toward the ground and the most recent traffic accident she's witnessed today. "I sure don't feel safe."

Égwen falls silent. Benkle waits for her to continue, but she doesn't seem to have anything else to say. He struggles to find words for himself, until Égwen speaks: "I haven't been able to bring myself to tell my family what's going on. I could really use some help."

Benkle says, "As soon as I've got another job, you'll have all my remaining time and energy, Égwen. You should know by now that I'm here for you."

"Of course," Égwen says, as they slip through the electroshielding of the middle tower garage. The maze of parked hovercars is five hundred deep. The concrete ceiling above them and columns around them are all painted steel gray. Every few columns down, their color and that of the ceiling changes with sharp dividing lines. "Which section did you park in?" Égwen asks.

Benkle says, "East Green 5." The vehicle automatically turns left. "I will never forget that smell." Benkle's lips purse in disgust bordering on nausea, then immediately turning into nausea. "I bet it's"—he dry heaves—"saturated my car."

Égwen slams on the breaks. "I'm sorry," she says, covering her mouth. "I need you to get out here if you are going to do that."

"I've got it," Benkle says, turning his thoughts to his boyfriend, whom he will see very soon. "I've got it."

"Are you sure?" Égwen asks. The hovertruck behind them honks over the shortwave radio.

Benkle backs away from her as best he can in his harness. "Yes." They are near the threshold where the color of the ceiling and the concrete columns changes from gray to deep blue.

Égwen looks Benkle over for a moment. The penguin in the hovertruck behind them honks again. "Good," Égwen says, and she pushes on the button marked "Proceed to East Green 5 Parking Garage." The hovercar moves.

Égwen says, "By the way, I'm sorry about how I treated you before all this shit really started going down."

"I figured it was something Huck did."

"It was something Huck did," Égwen confirms. Her face contorts in shame as she follows that up. "And I kind of saw him every time I looked at you."

"Glad to be putting a stop to that association!" Benkle says.

Égwen says, "I bet!" and she glances at him out the side of her eyes.

They reach the boundary where one half of a column is deep blue and the next is forest green. Benkle's lighter, fae-green econoluxury hovercar is just a few cars in. It's sandwiched between two crooked-parked Homvery personal tanks, which themselves would prevent Benkle's escape with his vehicle, even if not for the bright-yellow police-issue hoverlock weighing it to the floor with the force of a few hundred thousand tons.

Égwen grits her teeth and asks, "You want a lift somewhere?"

"Thanks," Benkle says. "Just let me grab something from my car."

CHAPTER 9: THE CURSE OF THE CANTANKEROUS ASSHOLE

Benkle knocks on a particleboard door in a chartreuse-colored hall. He adjusts his top hat on his head, and he taps his foot nervously. He glances down at his pants. The side of his leg has a large dirt stain left over from either his trip to Diadox or the one to Gravita. He wipes at it with his palm, and the door opens.

"Hey there, handsome," Alfounz says, opening the door to let Benkle in. Benkle approaches with wide arms to hug the taller man for a few long, deep breaths. Alfounz has sharp features, a strong freshly-shaven jaw, and muscles that bulge even at rest. His long black hair cascades down past his collar bones.

Alfounz's face contorts in anguish, and he says, "I can't believe my nephew's godfather is dead." He sobs quietly into Benkle's hat, and Benkle takes a moment to figure out what's going on and another to consider breaking away, before he gives in and sobs into Alfounz's chest.

Alfounz says, "Poor Bort."

"Poor Bort," Benkle says. He pushes Alfounz back and closes the door behind him.

Benkle stands and admires his boyfriend for a few seconds. Alfounz is in a black mostly unbuttoned, long-sleeved shirt and tight pink jeans. His pecs and his package all bulge. Benkle says, "How did I ever find you, my love?" as he runs his finger up Alfounz's chest.

Alfounz says, "Why don't you have a seat, babe, watch some television, and I'll be done in the kitchen in just a few minutes. I got that recipe from Ormr that you liked so much, and I'm trying it out now. I better get back to it before it burns."

Benkle's boyfriend says, "TV on," and a squat black pyramid on the floor lights up with colors, and a hologram appears, filling half the small living room with almost-full-sized holographic people, and an almost-complete holographic couch, sticking out of the floral-papered wall.

"It's Lip Heldinger!" Benkle squeals at the umber-skinned hologram of a man in a black top hat between a canary-yellow-colored man and woman who could easily be siblings, but are legally required not to be. They're probably cousins. Benkle asks himself out loud, "Aren't we all cousins?"

"What was that?" Alfounz asks, sticking his head out of the kitchen.

"Nothing!" Benkle shouts. Benkle and the hologram of Lip Heldinger lay back. The yellow people remove their yellow robes, revealing taut, naked, yellow bodies underneath, and they slowly drop to hands and knees. They crawl at a teasing pace toward Lip.

Benkle looks over his shoulder. "You know," he hollers across the apartment, "I'm not really that hungry."

"That's fine," Alfounz shouts. "Ormr said that this stuff keeps really well. I'm almost done. Then I'll come right in."

After a few minutes of waiting and heavy holographic petting, Lip's and Benkle's pants are both off, although Benkle's still wearing his baby-blue-and-black-plaid boxers. He struggles to see past the yellow woman to look at what Lip and the yellow man are doing. Alfounz comes into the room and sits next to Benkle on the couch, pressing up against his back, while Benkle stares at the scene playing out before them. Alfounz reaches around, but Benkle puts his hand around Alfounz's wrist.

"I've given so much of my time to that company," Benkle says, turning to face his lover. "I've given my body to that cruelly designed furniture, I've risked my life for that company, and with the wizard sickness, I've sacrificed my own mind. I gave my soul to these people, and what did I get in return?"

Alfounz can only embrace Benkle with a sympathetic look on that gorgeous face of his.

Benkle squeezes Alfounz, saying, "If that's the cost of money, I don't think I want it anymore."

Alfounz looks Benkle in the eyes and kisses him with enormous passion and barely held control. They lie back and enjoy the show for a moment. Heldinger is standing up now, driving himself into the yellow man, who is bent over the holographic couch, and the yellow woman sucks on Lip's finger.

Benkle glances around and says, "I forgot how dingy your apartment is." Alfounz pushes away from Benkle. "What?" Benkle asks. "Don't shit yourself while you're away from your spare pants."

Alfounz crosses his arms, muttering, "That doesn't make any sense, you cantankerous asshole."

A huddled figure squats behind a broken wall

in a fallen building. They're looking through a very old, cracked pair of binoculars and through the permanently orange-tinted air. A line of smoke rises from the next hill over. Blackened, burnt, long-dead trees dot the landscape, between the equally frequent white, glass trees. Hardy, toxic, radiation-resistant fungus grows from the corpses of the true trees. The dawn light is a hazy pink in the east. Stars still shine weakly through the radioactive haze that colors the air orange.

The figure wears a large gas mask that looks like oversized oval goggles over a dull steel microphone. Layers of rubber melted over flame-retardant fabrics into a thick shroud cover her from hood to hem. Over her shroud, mythral scale mail surrounds her abdomen. A symbol not unlike a capital D with a plus sign in the middle, drawn in blood on the back of her armor, indicates to other Dwellers that she is part of their clan.

On another hill across the shallow valley, breaks in the line of rising smoke indicate a hidden message. "It's done. If we survive the next week, I'll smoke you again then."

"Ugh," the Dweller says under her breath. She puts her pen and waxed paper in a pocket of her backpack and pulls a couple other pieces of paper out. "I hate getting up this early."

Written on one of the papers in Dweller script is a foraging list:

Raeya, please obtain as many as you can of the following before your morning meeting: ten days' rations, ammo, drink water, and an old unit of trade called a coin. I need you to get a message for me at dawn. Climb Elm Street Hill and look across the valley. Bring your telescope. Please pull San aside at the meeting and give him the accompanying note. Ask him what a coin is if you don't know. Get as many of these items as you can to prepare for the expedition, and at least one coin per forager. -Garc

The other note says

Ulledes needs to know that his father passed away in an accident at his lab. Pull him aside and tell him in private, and then send him back to the bunker with the

*message Raeya got for me.
The hunt for the gianter
kobold is off. The team has
a new mission. Go to the
bunker of the Polypods,
and do whatever it takes to
get Dr. Trebor here to finish
Ulledes Sr.'s work. -Garc*

Raeya looks at the amorphous pink glow that is the sun shining through Vədtorscape's radioactive atmosphere as it just barely rises above the horizon between two hills. "And now I'm late. Damn Garc. He needs to start getting his own messages."

A small round metal object glints in the dawn light, until the shadow of a winged rat passes over it. It's emaciated, but still the beast is almost half again as massive as Raeya, with white fur and long blood-covered jaws. It has oversized red eyes and long, perky ears. It wears a stained gray suit with short, wide wing-sleeves, and a red bowtie. Fur pokes out through the tears and cuts in the creature's suit. Radiation lesions dot the creature's fur.

Raeya stops, and backs away slowly. She tells herself, *Ratbirds tend to eat other rats, so I should be fine. I better stay silent in case it's a ratbat, though, or just a really hungry ratbird.* She clings to the wall. *What if it's a ratsect? Whatever it is, stay absolutely silent, Raeya, and don't you* dare *produce a smell.*

The winged, suited rat-person sniffs the air and turns. As its shadow follows, the glint on the ground returns, and the beast approaches Raeya where she hides, just around a corner, backpack and right side against the wall, arm against the wall, breathing maybe a little too heavily.

The beast leaps into the air and flies toward the sunrise, and the source of the smoke rising on Lorel Hill.

Raeya steps into a small partially intact shack in the middle of a sea of fallen skyscrapers. The ground is entirely composed of rubble, and the shack is floored with smaller rubble and filled with Raeya's impatiently waiting team. Each has a different kind of gas mask, and a unique earth-toned suit made of layers of melted rubber, with the dweller symbol drawn in blood on the back. Most of them have cuts in their suits, leading into a core of fibrous metal used to block some of the radiation inherent in the atmosphere of Vədtorscape. They stand around a small table covered in a large hand-drawn map of the greater metropolitan area and all the fallen skyscrapers.

San, the Forage Master, says, "You're late."

Ulledes says, "I did what you suggested, Raeya."

San and Ulledes turn to look at each other.

Ulledes says, "And now my ant farm is thriving."

"Good," Raeya says.

Ulledes says, "And my father loves them. So much protein."

"Oh . . ."

San says, "You two can talk about your gross bug farms later. We have a gianter kobold to kill, and less time to do it, thanks to your tardiness. The meeting starts now."

"Actually," Raeya says, "can I speak with you alone for just a moment, San?"

He says, "Absolutely not. You've delayed us enough already. Maybe if you would get up at a reasonable hour, this wouldn't be happening, but here we are, and we've got no time for any of your shit."

"I've been out foraging while the rest of *you* were sleeping," she says, pointing at San and the Dwellers nearest to him, "and I got some cool shit, including an ancient coin. It's dated 2525. The language is archaic, but I believe it's commemorating one of the more recent times the world did not end."

"Really?" San says. "That's the least interesting thing there is on the surface, and you really shouldn't go out alone. There is absolutely no reason to."

Raeya says, "There are a ton of reasons, one in particular I'd like to share with you in private."

"Name one," San says, "here in front of everybody."

"I . . ." Raeya cocks her head. "There are so many reasons, I should just be able to pull one out of my ass." She gestures as if to do so. "They're just getting stuck, like a bunch of people trying to go through a door at the same time, but the door is my anus."

"Enough," San says. "Raeya, Faoris, you two are scouting today, so listen well. You won't get a chance to ask me any questions."

"Yes sir!" A youthful voice coming from a Dweller no more than four feet tall is muffled by a canister-type gas mask they wear.

"Keep your voice down," San whispers, holding a finger up to his gas mask.

Raeya steps over toward San and says, "I really think you should let me speak to you in private."

San says, "I am in charge here, and I'll tell you when we need to speak in private!"

Raeya says, "I have these notes from—"

San waves his hand in a dismissive gesture. "I don't care what else you have in your backpack! Ulledes, show us what *you* have in *your* backpack."

Ulledes pulls his bag off his shoulders and puts it on the ground. He pulls the zipper down and puts his hand inside. He pulls a short rod out and puts it on top of the map on the table between them. One side ends in a short, thick wire wrapped in electrical tape, and a four-pronged power coupling. The other end splits in two and has twin blades.

"It's called an electromagnetic bident. This is Ulledes Sr.'s response to what happened at the Humble Celebration."

Ulledes presses a button on the side of the rod, and it telescopes into a weapon twice as tall as any of them.

"What's the point of that?" the shortest Dweller asks. "And wouldn't a shorter name be better?"

Ulledes pulls a car battery out of his bag. "Sparkspork?" he asks. The battery is connected to a power coupling that fits the one at the end of the electromagnetic bident.

"We'll work out the name on the trip," San says. "Each of you will get one of these when we return from our first trip out. When we find the gianter kobold, we'll hook up these sparksporks— I think I like that one. We'll hook up these sparksporks and brace for impact. The monster will attack and impale itself on these things."

"Sir," Raeya says, "I think you really want to see what I've got for you."

"No time," San says, "because we've got to hoof it to the bunker of the Three-Fingers to get the batteries to power the rest of these things. They have agreed to give us the batteries we need if we take care of a certain radioactive mutant with a certain helicopter."

"That fuck?" Ulledes asks.

"That fuck indeed," San says. "He's been spotted by Three-Fingers flying to Balus Hill. We'll be joined by some of their finest scavengers, and then we're all going to have to split up to search for the asshole in the helicopter. Whoever sees them will move a kilometer away, send a smoke signal, and hide a kilometer north of that location, where everyone will converge."

"Then, once we've regrouped, we'll attack. One of you will probably die, if not a few of you, but we WILL kill that bastard! Then we'll be heroes to our people, and to the Three-Fingers. All except for Raeya, probably." Everyone turns to look at Raeya, whose arms are folded in front of her.

"We're going to steal their helicopter and fly it back to the Three-Fingers' bunker. They will then trade the helicopter for the batteries we need to make our bidents—er, sparksporks work, and a year's supply of dried rat meat. By then it'll be their new-year celebration." San raises his voice ever so slightly. "That's when it's time to party!"

The group pats their shrouds in a quiet cheer.

"When we return from the Three-Finger clan, we'll have the batteries necessary to kill the gianter kobold," San says. "Some of you will probably die, if not most of you, but we WILL kill the beast!"

"We'll all be double heroes to every bunker for a hundred miles, and Garc will make me a full Forage Master."

A breeze knocks the door against its frame, until Faoris latches it closed. Raeya pulls three pieces of paper out of her bag and holds them out to San. Ulledes and Faoris turn their masks toward Raeya. Raeya waves her papers, trying to get his attention.

San turns around and continues on as if Raeya wasn't doing anything. "Faoris, you and Raeya need to head out now." He steps up to a windowsill with half a pane left, and into pink light. "The rest of us will meet back here and leave in three hours."

Faoris moves to leave, but Raeya grabs him by the backpack.

"Let go of me."

"RAEYA!" San raises his voice. "You *will* follow my orders!"

Raeya tells Faoris, "Don't go just yet."

"Do you want to let the gianter kobold keep on rampaging?"

"Of course not," Raeya says. "Who would want th—"

"You seem to," San says, "what with your constant sedition today."

"What?" Raeya asks. "What do you mean?"

San slams his fists down on the table. "Obey your leader and get the fuck out of here!" He points at the door.

"Can we speak privately for a moment?" Raeya asks.

"No," San says. "Now go, before I have you martialled and turned into Vədtorscapian Humble Pie." San draws a long, curved knife from beneath his cloak.

Raeya puts her hands on her hips.

The whole room looks back and forth between Raeya and San.

A warm wind creeps through a small hole in the door, making it whistle.

Raeya sighs and says, "Garc told me to go up top. I have these notes from Garc. One for you, one for me." She slips her backpack off and reaches into a pocket. "The list of stuff I showed you." She pulls a piece of paper out. "This note is for you."

"Let me see that." San snatches it from Raeya's hand.

San reads aloud. "Ulledes needs to know that his father passed away in an accident at his lab. Pull him aside and tell him in private . . ." San puts the note down. "Why didn't you take me aside and give this to me in private? "

"I tried to!" Raeya says, flailing her arms in exasperation.

"She did," Ulledes says, as if in shock.

"Yeah," Faoris agrees.

"Repeatedly," Ulledes says, and then, with anger growing in his voice, Ulledes repeats, "*Repeatedly*."

The group leader puts his hands on the table and yells, "You should *not* have gone out alone, Raeya! Garc knows I don't trust you. He never should have sent *you*, and you definitely shouldn't have gone out alone!"

Raeya crosses her arms and says, "You shouldn't yell."

"Why not?" San says, malice filling his voice.

"You know why," Raeya says. She puts her hand up. "And by the way, Garc told me—"

An emaciated flying-rat creature swoops in through the window behind the group leader, wraps its back claws around San's waist, and carries him out the window before any of them can react at all. The remaining Dwellers grab their shit and run.

To be continued . . .

hopefully.

Appendices

Appendix I: Creatures

Alfounz - alfänz. Terranoid human. Lover of Benkle.

Amazons - aməzänz. Humans from six to twelve feet tall from the planet Amazonia, who reproduce solely through parthenogenesis.

Benkle Cherryblossum - biNGk(ə)l CHerēbläsəm. Terranoid Executive Assistant to the President of Solscapes Interstellar Realty.

Birdcrabs - bərdkrabz. Offshoots of birds that look like crabs.

Bish-hop of Ihs - biSHhäp əv is. Scapi warrior-CEO from Metrofedilis.

Bort - bôrt. Assistant to the Vice President of Casting at Solscapes Interstellar Realty.

Brance Heldinger - brans heldiNGər. Terranoid musician, famous on Monric and across the Star Cluster.

Cave Anglers - kāvaNGglərz. Cavernous Anglers. Angler fish that evolved into giant amphibious cave dwellers.

Cotl - kätl. Excellonian gnome. Closing coordinator for Solscapes Interstellar Realty. Practical joker.

Devi - dēvē. A uniquely variable species from Stonis.

Dragonmade - dragənmād. Typically humanoid creatures genetically engineered or transmuted to have dragon DNA, and their descendants.

Dragons - dragənz. Usually winged, scaly, carnivorous creatures that are known for their elemental breath weapons, massive size, diversity, and extreme longevity.

Dr. Hedra Nalyaci - däktər hēdrə nôlyäsē. Excellonian terranoid. Wizard First Class, Rainbow Wizard, and Vice President of Casting at Solscapes Interstellar Realty.

Dr. K. - däktər kā. Excellonian terranoid. Polymath and Head Engineer at Solscapes Interstellar Realty.

Dr. Mit Ritter - däktər mit ritər. Excellonian terranoid. Protectist First Class and owner of Mit Ritter's Emporium of Life, formerly the Gær Tower Clinic. Avoid at all costs.

Dinocrabs - dīnōkrabz. An offshoot of dinosaurs that look like crabs.

Dweller Clan - dwelər klan. A Vədtorscapian clan

from the Peiuhqt Bunker.

Égwen Bideon - ēgwin bidēän. Excellonian terranoid. Employee Resources Director at Solscapes Interstellar Realty.

Elecres - ēlekrēz. Electron creatures. Originally part of an ancient video game, these creatures are magically supported in the Material Realms, and disappear if magic ever fails. Elecres change form with changes in their emotions. Most have abrupt, total changes in form and function, while a few express specific traits by degree, for example, growing horns with rising anger, or becoming less solid with sadness.

Elementals - eləmentlz. The creatures from the Elementus star system and their descendants. Those who aren't heavily composed of a single element or compound in their keratin and collagen are sometimes referred to as flesh elementals or pseudoelementals.

Ent - ənt. Treant. Vaguely humanoid trees.

Excellonians - eksəlōnēənz. The people of the city of Excellon. Most are human, arachian, or anarachian, like anywhere on Monric, but Excellon is both the most densely populated and the most diverse city on the moon.

Faoris - fāôris. Vədtorscapian of the Dweller clan.

Fishcrabs - A species of catfish that look kind of like crabs and kind of like rocks.

Faeish - fāiSH. Faeish. Creatures from the moon Fae. Some are talking animals, others are offshoots of humanity, still others are the descendants of Elemental migrants. They typically regenerate, and many have chlorophyll, making their skin and/or hair green. Faeish are stereotyped as being carriers of disease.

Ferele - ferelə. Terranoid Translocationist and Realtor Wizard, employed by Solscapes Interstellar Realty.

Flora - flôrə. Part stonisi, part haliti, Executive Assistant to Mrs. Lotterydale at Solscapes Interstellar Realty.

Ferele Miden - ferelə m. Terranoid Translocationist and Realtor Wizard, employed by Solscapes Interstellar Realty.

Followers of Fate - fälōərz əv fāt. A Xolish religious group that worships the triumvirate deity Destiny above all others.

Forage Master - fôrij mastər. The title of the leaders of Dweller scavenger parties.

Gianter Kobold - jīəntər kōbôld. A kobold that's even

bigger than a giant kobold, but not as big as the giantest kobold.

Huck Lotterydale - hək lädərēdāl. Excellonian terranoid President of Solscapes Interstellar Realty. Perhaps the most pathetic human being in the known universe.

Human - (h)yo͞omən. Bipedal primates that usually have some amount of alopecia, and little to no tail. Humans are considered one of the most invasive groups of species in the star cluster.

Humanoid - (h)yo͞omənoid. Due to the invasiveness of human species, any four-limbed biped, primate, or even vaguely human-like species is sometimes referred to as humanoid. Goblinoids are often considered humanoids, but not vice versa, except on the Kaeris Branch of Fae's World Tree.

Hurrasi - həräsē. Terranoids native to the Thronelands

Ihsish - isiSH. Scapi terranoids who migrated to Dragonthrone. They are stereotypically greedy, self-serving cronyists.

Jam - ẇmʐʐiškaÞį ɹᶲᶲį. Executive Employee Resources Assistant at Solscapes Interstellar Realty. Species unknown.

Khen - khen. Some sort of teal terranoid living in New Old Excellon.

Lip Heldinger - lip heldiNGər. Terranoid known most famously for being the son of aging gigapop star, Brance Heldinger, secondly for his porn.

Lizardcrabs - lizərdkrabz. Lizards that look like crabs.

Mammalcrabs - maməlkrabz. Mammals that look like crabs.

Mrs. Lotterydale - misiz lädərēdāl. Terranoid owner and CEO of Solscapes Interstellar Realty.

Myrmidons - mərmədänz. Mobile ant colonies that use found objects, usually twigs, to build colony-wide carapaces. These carapaces normally take at least a vaguely humanoid form. The intelligence of the queen is exceedingly variable, but they are all highly social creatures. Stereotyped as infantile as this species is only a thousand years old.

Monrician - mônriSHən. The creatures of Monric, mostly human and anarachian, or, alternately, their food that isn't shipped from off-world. Stereotyped as selfish, rude elitists.

Mrs. Lotterydale - misiz lädərēdāl. Terranoid owner and CEO of Solscapes Interstellar Realty.

Ogres - ōgərz. Large, muscular goblinoids that evolved on Fae, with more terranoid-like facial features. Stereotyped as wanna-be humans and brutes.

Ormr - ôrmir. A purple dragonmade and head chef at the Solscapes Tower Executive Cafe.

Pandacrabs - A variety of furry, black-and-white crabs descended from pandas.

Primists - One of many groups of Primal Pantheon worshippers claiming to know the true and un-altered story of the ancient, dead gods.

Poyo - pōyō. Huck's pet elecre and confidant.

Raeya - Vədtorscapian forager of the Dweller clan.

Reine - rinə. Myrmidon accountant for Solscapes Interstellar Realty.

Ren Peerclay - ren pirklā. Excellonian terranoid Rainbow Wizard, and Wizard Second Class.

Robots - rōbätz. Autonomous machines that often claim to be modeled after the original lifeforms.

San - san. Junior Forage Master, leader of the second most elite team of War Foragers in the Dweller clan.

Scapi - skāpē. Vədtorscapian terranoids and ko-bolds of Dragonthrone. Stereotyped as pompous cutthroats.

Sea Bats - sēbatz. Semi-aquatic diurnal bats that mostly feed off of fish.

Stonisi - stōnēsē. Stonesbreaki, *archaic*. People from Stonis. Primarily flesh elementals. Often the word specifically refers to the terranoids from Stonis, who tend to have metallic hair and tapeta lucida. With intermixing, the Stonisi come as small as brownies and as large as giants. Stereotyped as con artists, bandits, and thieves.

Terranoids - terənoidz. Humans that grow from two to ten feet tall. Terranoids often call themselves the "standard humans." Stereotypical characteristics include childish narcissism, denial about all aspects of their lives, and unfettered xenophobia.

The Fly Society - THə flī səsīədē. A secret society of bottom-tier Monrician oligarchs.

The Impotent - THə impōtənt. A derogatory phrase used by the upper class and their cronies to describe the huddled masses living in the shadow of those that steal and hoard wealth, magic, technology, and power.

Three Finger Clan - THrē fiNGgər klan. A Vədtorscapian clan with only three fingers on each hand.

Throni - T̲Hrōnē. Thronelander. The people of Dragonthrone to people who do not live on Dragonthrone. To people who live on Dragonthrone, a Throni or Thronelander is a person of the Thronelands continent, while thronelanders call themselves Godslanders, and their continent Godslands. Stereotyped as pompous holy book thumpers.

Tree Gnomes - trē nōmz. A hybrid of gnomes and elves that are typically one-half inch to five inches tall. Stereotypes for tree gnomes center around baking.

Ulledes - yo͞olədəs. Vədtorscapian War Forager and Tinkerer's Apprentice in the Dweller Clan.

Vədtorscapians - vetôrskāpēəns. Radioactive mutants. The kobolds and terranoids that remain on Vədtorscape after the world caught on fire, as well as their offshoot species.

Ⓓavid - T̲Hə ten THouz(ə)nTH āvid. A Diadoxian realtor for Solscapes Interstellar Realty.

Appendix II: Locations

Amazonia, Xol - Amazon. A high-gravity planet inhabited solely by tall, human women who breed parthenogenetically.

Antigul Nebula - An oddly dense red nebula hundreds of light years across, into which the Solscapes and all the nearby solar systems are falling.

Balus Hill, Vədtorscape, The Far Realms - The Balus Glass Forest. A desolate hill covered in blackened, dead palm trees with their roots exposed and the vaguely tree-like white glass. The glass was left behind in once-sandy spots, where lightning struck before the ocean dissapeared and the sand was swept away in the radioactive winds to be replaced by even more-radioactive dust.

Dragonthrone, Elementus - Moon of Gravita and epicenter of the Dragon Wars of Succession. The most diverse world in Elementus since Stonis flooded.

Elecre Worlds - EWs. Virtual worlds created predominantly by the ancient Monricians.

Excellon, Monric, Xol - The oldest megacity on Monric.

Fae, Xol - Fae, *archaic*. The first moon of Primordo, famous across the star cluster for its World Tree, the only one of its kind in the Material Realms. The moon is now gravitationally locked to Primordo, and the World Tree spins and wobbles when sister moon Monric gets too close.

Greensville, Gravita, Elementus - A village of Primordians and Amazons just south of the Lowest Golden Valley, but still part of the Feudal Monarchy of the Lowest Golden Valley.

Ihs, Dragonthrone, Elementus - A heavily-populated, especially human country. Ihs is the skyscraper-filled home of the vast majority of the Scapi people, right in the middle of a low-tech, very magic-dependent Thronelands continent. The Scapi built Ihs after they fled from their ancestral home world of Vədtorscape, when it caught on fire.

L Town Twee, Diadox, Galalos - A small dongus factory town in East Ωex.

L Town Twee Lake, Diadox, Galalos - A lake infested with gonorrhea-17b at the outskirts of L Town Twee.

Maledis - A red giant star with a system populated mostly by daemons and dead assholes.

Maybe River, Diadox, Galalos - A glacier fed creek running into the L Town Twee Lake. Believed to be the primary source of the lake's gonorrhea infestation.

Monric, Xol - Mônric, *archaic*. The Half-World. The low-atmosphere, high-tech second moon of Primordo. Monric is so densely populated that skyscrapers are the most common sort of building, and the vast majority of the food is shipped in from Fae and Primordo.

New Old Excellon City, Monric, Xol - Noec. A region at the heart of Excellon. Considered to have the second oldest and the least well kept infrastructure on the moon.

Solscapes Tower - The single largest fire hazard in the known multiverse.

Stonis, Elementus - Stonesbreak, *archaic*. Moon of Gravita. Homeworld of the so-called flesh elementals. Stonis is the most habitable world for humans in Elementus, but after the flood, the crouds of the single remaining continent forced many creatures to flee to Dragonthrone, the only other habitable place in the system for humans and flesh elementals.

The Feudal Monarchy of the Lowest Golden Valley, Gravita, Elementus - A valley made primarily of gold, populated primarily by golden elementals.

The Glass Forest, Dragonthrone, Elementus - A vast region of the Hurassi Desert in the northern Thronelands, known for the glass pillars made from sand that was struck by lightning. The glass forest is sacred to certain Hurrasi tribes, and cursed to others.

The Heavenly Star - A white dwarf star mostly populated by angels, archons, retirees, and narcissistic fuckboys that do nothing but party and scam the old people.

The Solscapes - The star cluster. The Living Systems, The Colonized Worlds. A growing system of inhabited celestial bodies and pocket dimensions.

Thronelands, Gravita, Elementus - Godslands. The largest continent of Dragonthrone, home of Throne Mountain, and the Throne of Dragons. More humans live in the Thronelands than on any other island or region of the moon.

Vədtorscape, The Far Realms - Once this was the only habitable world in the Far Realms for organisms who were not from the Far Realms. It was home to terranoids and many, many varieties of kobold, before the ourstorical records say it caught fire.

Vinsrock, Stonis, Elementus - A feudalist dwarven territory in the north of Stonis' single continent.

Xol - A yellow dwarf star.

Appendix III: Colors of Magic

Black - Protectis. Healing and Protection magic.

White - Mortua. Death and undeath. Restricted to necroscopy by interstellar and divine laws.

Red - Subtractive. Destruction magic.

Orange - Conjuration. Creation magic.

Yellow - Psionic. Clairvoyance, telepathy, and mind control. Only legal in Moneyist and Feudal societies.

Green - Naturalis. Manipulation of non-sentient and low-sentience creatures.

Blue - Translocation. Teleportation and movement magic.

Violet - Transmutation. Change in form and function.

Brown - Elemental. Tempestri, pyromancy, cryomancy, as well as sonic, void, and earth magic.

Appendix IV: Deities

Adarayan Pantheon - An ancient, long-dead pantheon attributed with creating life in the star cluster. Adarayans claim that she was the mother of Prime, and she lived long after he died spending her final centuries cleaning up her son's messes.

Destiny - Fate. The Fates. The triumvirate head of the Pantheon of Fate, the most powerful group of deities in the Living Systems, with the possible exception of the Shadow Lords. Destiny consists of the goddess of magic, the god of time, and the deity of death.

Primal Pantheon - An ancient, long-dead pantheon attributed with creating life in the star cluster. Adherents often claim that Prime, the head of the pantheon, was the father-husband of Adaraya.

The Protector - An ourstorically Monrician deity, forced to leave after the Divine Aide Act was signed into law. Her whereabouts are currently unknown.

The Shadow Lords - A group of deities that rule over the Shadow Realms, worlds that purportedly traveled interstellar space at the pantheon's behest and now orbit the Nexus Star. They claim to be the oldest living deities, and various Adarayans and Primalists and Shadow Worshippers alike claim the Shadow Lords to be the long-lost children of Prime.

Appendix V: Terms and Things

BrilliantEats - A common vender brand on Monric, specializing in knocking off other brands and making their products marginally healthier.

Claw Fin - A claw that's evolved from a fin.

Decillion - A criminally irresponsible amount to hoard, when referring to currency or most other things.

Drink Water - Water on Vədtorscape that is not toxic to drink—at least to Vədtorscapians.

Duck - The post-autocorrect form of the word *fuck*. Duck is used to convey a mild need for an expletive, or a genuine need for an expletive, by people who are conditioned not to swear.

Dumpstercar - A hovercar made from parts found primarily in the trash.

Electromagnetic bident - Sparkspork. A Dweller Clan weapon made to combat the gianter kobolds, designed to impale and electrocute simultaneously.

Humble Celebration - Flesh Party. A party thrown by many Vədtorscapian clans in the event they are consuming Vədtorscapian Humble Pie.

Homvery - Manufacturers of personal combat vehicles that run exclusively on fossil fuels or nuclear fusion.

Leg Fin - Fins that have evolved into legs and sometimes penises.

MeTube - A website for narcissists to upload their holovideos.

Mythral - An unusual spelling for an unusual substance.

Penistache - A mustache composed of penises or penis-like objects, or a mustache that is shaped like one or more penises.

Robopass - A sticker that can be purchased for less than top-end vehicles that automatically bills for entrance fees and prevents the destruction of the vehicle with the rider in it by automated security.

Sorcerer - The title given to people who learn magic in their dreams or cast it instinctively.

Sorcerers - A card game popular across the star cluster.

Sosocial App - A social media app designed to replace the apps that replaced socialization.

Spectrum Wizard - Polycaster. Mixcaster. Rainbow

Wizard. A wizard who can effectively cast at least three colors of magic. Most definitions require four or five, while many require that the caster be able to effectively wield at least six of the colors of magic. Having the ability to cast seven or more gives the caster a *The* at the beginning of the title.

Solscapes Interstellar Realty - A small realty company with headquarters in the 4§ region of New Old Excellon City, Monric.

solscapesmultiverse.com - The second least popular website in the known universe.

Treebacon - Bacon grown on a genetically altered tree, distributed by the pet food company Meat Cereal Inc.

Vigillion - More money than most gods have, or roughly the number of jelly beans in the largest jelly bean guessing game ever.

Wizard - A catchall term for any magic caster who learns their trade through study, be it of standard drawing, gesture casting, evocation, or runic casting. Some people define a wizard specifically as a graduate of one of the Orega Schools of Magic.

Wizard First Class - A graduate, with highest honors, of one of the Orega Schools of Magic.

Wizard Second Class - A graduate, with high honors, of one of the Orega Schools of Magic.

Wizard Third Class - A graduate, with honors, of one of the Orega Schools of Magic.

Wizard Sickness - The Corruption of Magic. The Taint. A recently discovered affliction affecting casters of magic, poisoning their minds. Its full list of symptoms, spread, and its cause have all yet to be identified. There is no known cure.

World Tree - A tree that uses the span of an entire celestial body to feed its roots, and branches out to fill a space similar to its world in breadth. While they are a common feature of celestial bodies within the Fairy Domains, only one World Tree exists in the Material Planes, that of Fae, which has heart-shaped, forest-green leaves that bear entire civilizations of wee folk and different fruit depending on the time of year and the elevation of the limb.

Worldwood - Wood made from a World Tree.

Xtie - A long bow tie that forms a large *X*.

Vədtorscapian Humble Pie - A meaty dish common across Vədtorscape.

Solscapes Will Return

in

9 798779 667302